Colorado Gold

IMPERIAL PUBLIC LIBRARY
P.O. BOX 307
IMPERIAL, TX 79743

*Also by Douglas Hirt
in Large Print:*

A Good Town
The Ordeal of Andy Dean
Able Gate
Devil's Wind

Colorado Gold

Douglas Hirt

Copyright © 1993 by Douglas Hirt

All rights reserved.

Published in 2004 by arrangement with Cherry Weiner Literary Agency.

Wheeler Large Print Western.

The text of this Large Print edition is unabridged.
Other aspects of the book may vary from the original edition.

Set in 16 pt. Plantin by Ramona Watson.

Printed in the United States on permanent paper.

Library of Congress Cataloging-in-Publication Data

Hirt, Douglas.
    Colorado gold / Douglas Hirt.
       p. cm.
      ISBN 1-58724-671-6 (lg. print : sc : alk. paper)
      1. Colorado River Valley (Colo.-Mexico) — Fiction.
2. Gold mines and mining — Fiction.   3. Arizona — Fiction.   4. Large type books.   I. Title.
PS3558.I727C65 2004
813'.54—dc22   2004041932

This book is dedicated to Donald Hamilton, a storyteller without equal, from a once-upon-a-time college student in Santa Fe, New Mexico, who filled late dorm hours with the adventures of Matt Helm — another Santa Fean. Thank you!

National Association for Visually Handicapped
serving the partially seeing

As the Founder/CEO of NAVH, the only national health agency solely devoted to those who, although not totally blind, have an eye disease which could lead to serious visual impairment, I am pleased to recognize Thorndike Press* as one of the leading publishers in the large print field.

Founded in 1954 in San Francisco to prepare large print textbooks for partially seeing children, NAVH became the pioneer and standard setting agency in the preparation of large type.

Today, those publishers who meet our standards carry the prestigious "Seal of Approval" indicating high quality large print. We are delighted that Thorndike Press is one of the publishers whose titles meet these standards. We are also pleased to recognize the significant contribution Thorndike Press is making in this important and growing field.

Lorraine H. Marchi, L.H.D.
Founder/CEO
NAVH

* Thorndike Press encompasses the following imprints: Thorndike, Wheeler, Walker and Large Print Press.

A special thanks to Julie Ramirez and Luisa Graff for their help in translating my English into Spanish and adding a dash of south-of-the-border seasoning to the story.

1

Harrison Mandell slapped the back of his neck and grinned at the bloody smear on his palm. *You've become a vindictive SOB, Harry,* he mused.

The far-off whistle of the approaching Southern Pacific train brought his view around to the dingy window. The noise drifted up out of the desert like the urgent bellow of a month-old calf looking for a misplaced udder. A lonely sound in a dry, empty wasteland that a man could hear for fifty miles — if not in actual fact, then as an echo of something remembered as he stared out across the hot, flat desert.

The Southern Pacific tracks ran past the East Bank Saloon: two glistening streaks beneath the relentless sun. A heavy timber trestle carried them across the red-mud waters of the Colorado River where steamboats puffed and wheezed at their docks, and wide barges, piled high with supplies destined for the gulf, sat low in the water. Other than the ebb and swirl of the river, nothing moved under a blazing midday sun — nothing but an occasional Indian along the bluffs and the dusty cavalry troops of Fort Yuma over on the California side, going through their endless maneuvers.

Beyond Fort Yuma the rails curved west, and somewhere in that direction lay San Diego. A pleasant country — or so he had been told. Mandell made a wry grin. Considering where he had disembarked, and where he was going, he wasn't fully convinced anything on this end of the continent could be pleasant.

His thoughts went back to the cool mountains of Virginia, where he had been less than a month ago when the telegram arrived. The train had brought him to Chicago where a carriage pulled by two matched horses picked him up at the depot and carried him to the new white mansion Allan had built south of Chicago. Joan had met him at the door, slender in a long white dress that nearly matched the color of her hair. She looked weary.

"Harry," she said, giving him a hug and standing back to clasp him by the shoulders. "You look well. Tell me, have you gotten married yet?" She was teasing, of course, taking his left hand to examine the fingers there.

"Believe me, Joan, you and Allan will be the first to know."

"I don't believe that for an instant, but do promise me we won't be the very last."

William appeared at his mother's side and took Mandell's hand in a strong grip. "Harry. Good to see you again."

"I thought you were in New York?"

"I was. Bob is still there getting the new offices set up. I came back to help Mother."

Harrison's mouth drew a line of concern across his face. "How is Allan?"

Joan put on a brave face. "He has his bad days. He is no longer the 'Man of Iron,' as the newspapers used to call him. But he still works — most every day." She made a faltering smile. "If he didn't have the agency he would have withered long ago."

Harrison frowned. He had worked for Allan Pinkerton twelve years and had come to think of the Pinkertons as an extension of his own family. When his father died, Allan and Joan came to Colorado for the funeral even though Allan had been in the middle of a sensitive investigation. Allan was sixty-five now, and in failing health, and Harrison saw the strain his family was living under.

"I received Allan's telegram," he said.

William said, "Father has been waiting for you." He looked at his mother. "I'll take Harry back."

"We will talk later," Joan Pinkerton said, her blue eyes smiling bravely.

As they proceeded down the hallway to Allan's in-home office where he spent more and more of his time these days, William said, "We have had a communication from a mining company in Arizona. You ever been to Arizona, Harry?"

Mandell took his eyes from the paintings, awards, and mementos that lined the wall. "Been through it a time or two. From what little I have seen of the territory, I have no inclination to go back."

William Pinkerton grinned. They stopped at a door and he knocked. From the other side came a voice Harrison had grown to recognize as clearly as if it had belonged to his father.

"Aye? Come on inside." After over forty years in this country, Allan Pinkerton still retained his heavy Scottish accent.

William opened the door. "Harry is here."

"Aye! Good — good. Come on in, Harry. Have a chair." Allan rose weakly out of his own chair and clasped Harrison's hand. The grip was not what it had been only a year before.

William stayed until Harrison Mandell was settled and his father back behind the desk, then left. Allan Pinkerton looked haggard. His hair had thinned back, and his once-brown beard was now burdened with considerable gray, but his blue eyes still burned with a fierce intenseness of a man who loved his work — loved life.

Allan Pinkerton was never a man for small talk when business needed to be taken care of, and now he got to the point. "We've been in communication with a mining firm in the territory of Arizona. I immediately thought you to be the right operative for the job, considering your experience with the Molly Maguires and the strikes of '77."

"Another labor-management dispute, sir?"

Allan shook his head. "Nae, this is something different. It seems, being in such an isolated location, the mining company — it is named *Mina del Agua Mala* — pays most of its debts with postal money orders" — Allan paused for effect — "and a large number of them seem to be missing. . . ."

Mandell departed the mansion with a new assignment, a new cover, and a book under his arm that would tell him all about being a mining engineer — or at least he hoped so. He caught a train to Demming, New Mexico, where the Southern Pacific made connections with the Santa Fe. From there westward, hell seemed to come a little closer with each mile left behind.

And here he had been deposited. Yuma, Arizona! The very pit of Mephistopheles' domain.

"Another round, mister?"

Mandell turned away from the grimy window and grimaced at the bottom of the beer mug. "No, thanks." Warm beer was just one more annoyance of this place.

The bartender wandered off to inquire after another fellow's needs, seemingly unconcerned with the heat and the bugs, waving an arm like a horse swings its tail to bat away the flies. Mandell's elbows found a comfortable perch on the bar as he looked out across the shabby room. The few men in the saloon, scattered among tables as dried out as the land, were for the most part the same men he had seen here the day before . . . and the day before that . . .

And the beer had gotten no better either. He had hoped it might when weighed against the misery of the mounting days. The delay had begun to chip away at his usual well-fortified supply of patience. He found it easy to understand why in the last four days he'd stood on the sidelines of six disputes being solved in what Mandell was beginning to accept as an eminently practical bare-knuckle fashion.

He wiped his brow with a dusty coat sleeve and glanced out the window again. The Southern Pacific station was farther up the street, shriveling in the heat, all but abandoned at this hour of the day when, like himself, the local inhabitants lingered in any bit of shade they could find. Not that the shade made Yuma any more bearable — a hole in the ground might . . . a deep hole . . . if one could devise a scheme for keeping the mosquitoes at bay — but at least it was better than waiting out under the ceaseless sun. And waiting was something Harrison Mandell was getting a lot of practice at.

He heard another steam whistle, closer and higher pitched this time, and for an instant his heart quickened. Then his hopes wilted, as had his collar days earlier. It was the signal of a steamboat docking, not departing. Probably a boat of the *Southern Pacific Company*. It seemed to have minor items — such as arrival and departure schedules — well in hand. Unlike another company . . .

"I du'na think it is ours," said a bored voice at his right. By the accent, Mandell half imagined that Allan Pinkerton himself had showed up to look over his shoulder, but it wasn't the famous detective. Gilligan McPeevy stepped to the bar and placed an open valise atop it. McPeevy was waiting for the same boat. A rotund man with a worn-down, withered look about him. Mandell figured he would have discovered a similar countenance if he peered into a mirror — minus the beard and muttonchops, of course. McPeevy was shorter by five inches, but he more than amply filled out his at-one-time-white linen shirt. In deference to the heat, McPeevy had discarded the drooping collar and opened the top shirt button. His gray and green checked vest hung apart, and he'd rolled up his shirt sleeves to the elbows.

Turning back to his empty mug, Mandell

said, "That's the signal of one arriving." He glanced over. "You know, McPeevy, you remind me very much of someone."

"Is that good or bad?"

"Good."

"In that case, a beer, please," the Scotsman said, flagging down the bartender. "And one for my mining engineer friend here too."

Mandell put a hand over his mug but McPeevy insisted. "I'll not hear it. A man has got to keep himself well irrigated in this infernal heat. Besides, I du'na like drinking alone."

Mandell turned an eye around the saloon. "That hardly needs to be a concern here." His hand leaped for the fly that had lighted on his ear.

McPeevy patted his bald skull with a yellowed handkerchief and settled the travel-weary derby hat back in place. "Blasted heat," he said. The beers arrived warm, and without the least indication of a head. Mandell sipped the flat brew. McPeevy gulped down half before coming up for a breath. He sleeved his lips and flagged the barman again.

"Have ye a saucer, sir?" he inquired.

The bartender considered McPeevy narrowly, partly because a scar half closed his left eye. "A saucer?" Then he glanced at the valise and a small grin showed on the bumpy contours of his face. "Oh, you mean for the

King." He reached under the bar and set a flat dish before McPeevy.

"Now there, my darling. Ye need to keep yourself irrigated too," McPeevy said, gently lifting a big tomcat out of the valise. He spilled beer into the saucer.

Mandell scratched King Robert the Second behind the ear. The cat gave the beer a tentative sniff. A big paw stretched out, touched it, and immediately the cat began to lick the paw dry. The cat continued up his leg, rubbing it up and down behind his ear.

"Doesn't seem to care for it much," the bartender observed with only a passing interest.

McPeevy sighed.

Mandell grinned.

McPeevy said to the bartender, "I hear the climate is more suitable up the river."

"More suitable for what?" The bartender looked mildly confused. "Ain't nothing wrong with the weather we got here." He wandered away, wiping his hands on his dirty apron.

McPeevy glanced at Mandell. "The man likes it here!"

Mandell lifted his mug of beer, not really wanting any more of it. "No accounting —" His words ended abruptly.

Out on the hot street a woman had suddenly screamed.

Mandell shot a glance at McPeevy, set the mug down, and stepped to the batwing doors to peer over the top of them. McPeevy pushed through and stopped on the sidewalk outside. From the direction of the Southern Pacific Hotel, which was also the train depot, a woman was running toward them down the middle of the wide street, screaming, and waving her arms over her head in a panic.

Two things struck Harrison Mandell right off. First was her mass of fiery red hair that tumbled down her back and flowed in the wind as she ran. Hair that was sure to draw the attention of any man watching. That is, of course, if it hadn't been for the second item that Mandell also noticed.

The lady was stark naked!

2

The cause of the woman's distress was not immediately clear, and Mandell stepped out onto the sidewalk along with a growing number of other curious and concerned gents. She was well endowed and quite good-looking. He guessed her age to be late twenties. As she drew nearer with her arms bouncing frantically overhead and that high-pitched shriek piercing the air, he noted with some curiosity that her wide eyes seemed somehow pronounced, as if artificially darkened, and that she wore a bit more powder and lip coloring than would be considered tastefully decent.

The thought brought a grin to his face. Tastefully decent women didn't hightail it down the middle of a street wearing nothing but their birthday suit.

There began some sort of commotion back at the Southern Pacific Hotel where she had come from, and then it was suddenly disgorging itself of people, some stumbling out of doors, others diving through open windows. They were climbing over the porch railings into the street and running off in all directions — but they weren't running very far, drawing up after a few long strides to look back. Whatever had driven them out was more of a curiosity than a danger.

"Saints!" McPeevy said, watching the panic-driven Godiva coming down the street. What was it he saw in the Scotsman's face? Wide-eyed shock . . . or was it surprise? Mandell glanced back at the hotel in time to see the door burst open and an Indian on horseback ride out onto the porch. The horse did a couple of spins, and the Indian reeled upon its back, nearly toppling off. Dressed in nothing more than a breechclout, the Indian readjusted his listing attitude, overcorrected, tried again, then heeled his horse along the length of the porch, driving fleeing patrons ahead of him like scattering chickens in a road.

The Indian seemed to be hunting for something . . . or someone.

He spied the fleeing girl, wheeled about, and gave a long howling shriek, driving the horse down a flight of steps into the street.

Eeeee-aiaiai.

He rode drunkenly, slipping a bit off the side of the animal as he came plunging recklessly.

The woman looked over her shoulder, and her own shrieking rose a notch or two to join the cacophony of the fast-approaching Indian.

In a sweeping glance, Mandell saw to his

dismay that no one intended to help the woman. His hand reached under his coat — but then he stopped himself. It took a moment for the subtlety of the other events, those happening right around him, to make themselves clear — and when they did he glanced back just to be certain.

The men — those local to the town, that is — were smiling. No, not just smiling, some were beginning to chuckle. McPeevy still wore that frozen stare of a man seeing a ghost, but then, he had just arrived from Kansas City. The bartender came up beside them just then, and he was chuckling too.

Mandell made a rapid reassessment of the situation. The Indian was almost upon the woman now. Behind him, the bartender was saying, "Ol' Olley is up to his mischief again." Mandell gave the man a curious glance.

The roar of a shotgun bellowed in the hot air.

The Indian drew rein at the sound, fell forward onto the neck of the horse, pushed himself straight, got the animal clumsily turned around, and headed back the way he had come.

"Get the hell out of here, you drunken red bastard!" the man with the shotgun shouted. He stepped out into the street from a building across the way. "Get the hell out, and stay the hell out of my town!"

The crowd parted for the horse racing back toward the station, and as the animal scrambled over the Southern Pacific tracks and out into the desert, two other women came jogging up the street as fast as their tight dresses would allow.

The man with the shotgun stretched out a hand to snag the naked girl as she streaked past. Mandell allowed himself to be swept along with the crowd that circled about the sobbing redhead.

"Take it easy, miss. I sent that crazy Injun packin'. You're in no danger now," he was saying, trying to calm the squirming armful he had suddenly acquired, and looking just a little uncomfortable about it. He seemed uncertain where to let his hand light, and was plainly relieved when the two bustling women finally arrived to drape a purple robe over the woman's pink shoulders.

"It's all right now, dear," the older of the two women consoled, taking the trembling girl into her arms. She and her companion, a much younger and more attractive woman, bore a striking resemblance to this bare creature that had just brought half the town out from their midday dens. Not in any family way, Mandell decided after a moment of careful study. It was more in the details, and Mandell had an artist's eye for details. He noted their dresses — well, at least the two who wore dresses. Bright-red skirts with yellow trimmings. The older woman wore a beige ruffled blouse under an emerald-green sleeveless jacket. The younger was in pale yellow and gray. Their hair was curled and arranged in ringlets that hung down about their shoulders. And here the similarities became striking — eyes darkened with something like blue soot, cheeks blushed and powdered, lips painted a dull red with some sort of waxy substance that showed signs of cracking about the edges.

"There, there, it's all right, Darlinda," the older woman soothed. "I declare, that wild savage put a fright into all of us. Poor Mr. Decater went shrieking out the back door with his britches and boots in hand —" She paused suddenly, pushed the girl out at arm's length, and looked sternly at her. "He did pay you up front, didn't he?"

The girl managed a nod of her head and fell back into the older woman's ample bosoms while the third woman glanced nervously about, as if being seen out in the glaring daylight was somehow embarrassing. She said uneasily, "Let's get back to the hotel, Molly."

The man with the shotgun turned to the crowd, and that was when the glint of sunlight off an oval shield pinned to his white, collarless shirt caught Mandell's eye. "Mighty warm day for standing around in the street gawking," the sheriff said.

The throng started back to the saloon. Mandell heard the sheriff say in a lower voice meant only for the women, "I thought we had this all settled, Molly. I want you and your girls out of Yuma."

Still cradling Darlinda's head, Molly shot back, "We're waiting for passage north, Ben. Once on board, we'll be out of your hair. You just keep that crazy Indian away from Darlinda."

That seemed to be a persistent problem in Yuma Town, Mandell mused, passage north. He had paused only a moment longer to hear the rest, and in that moment he caught a glimpse of the peculiar expression on McPeevy's face as he looked at Darlinda, sort of distant and thoughtful, as if the Scotsman had suddenly been given a mighty problem to cipher.

The Southern Pacific whistle sounded again, close this time, the black smoke of its approach a smudge upon the sky beyond the river.

Mandell and McPeevy made their way back into the saloon. At the bar, Mandell discovered his beer mug empty and the saucer bone dry. McPeevy's mug was empty too, as was every other glass and mug that had been left on the bar when they had dashed out into the street.

McPeevy grinned up at him and nodded his head at the valise.

24

Mandell glanced inside. King Robert the Second was out cold, but he did seem to be wearing the most contented grin Mandell had ever seen — on a cat, that is.

3

The bartender had a face that had seen one too many arguments and had come out on the short end of most of them. But he was a friendly sort, and Mandell had learned early on that one or two carefully placed questions would elicit a very thorough, point-by-point answer from the fellow — so long as you kept buying drinks. He was the sort of man Mandell sought out whenever he landed in a new town, and although Yuma was only a stop along the way, he was stuck here, and he might as well make the most of it.

"No one seemed too surprised by what just happened out front," he said when the bartender brought by two fresh beers. "This sort of thing happen often?"

The bartender's face turned twice-ugly by the grin that came to it. "Never know what that crazy Quechan will do next."

"Quechan?" Mandell tasted his beer and stifled a grimace.

"Some folks call 'em Yumans, but Quechan is the proper name for 'em. That fellow, he's the chief's oldest son. The kid is crazy. The old chief must have fed him too much fire-water when he was a tyke — or maybe he just dropped him on the head once too often."

"You called him Olley."

"Short for his Injun name. Olley-quo-teqi . . . somethin' or 'nother. Anyway, Olley's what we call him for short. He's got what you might call a drinking problem."

"How does he get it? It's illegal to sell liquor to the natives."

The bartender gave Mandell a patronizing leer. "Where you from, mister?"

"Lately, from Denver. But I spend a lot of time traveling. If you wanted to get a letter to me, I have a box in Chicago."

McPeevy was listening with a look of vague interest — mostly he was poking a concerned finger into King Robert the Second's ribs and not getting any response.

"Chicago?" the bartender roared, and everyone in the saloon stopped what they were doing to see if something interesting was about to happen. When it didn't, they all went back to their warm beer and rotgut whiskey, and the bartender said, "Chicago is in Illinois — last I heard. And Denver in Colorado. Both are *states*. This here is Arizona, and we is a *territory*, and hope to God to stay that way!"

"You're likely to, at least until the government can figure out who owns what in this godforsaken place."

The bartender shot him a narrow stare. "The point is, we don't operate under the same set of laws as you folks up North do. We got us the cavalry not half a mile away, and they do frown on us selling spirituous liquors to them Quechans, but they're over in California — a *state!* We say 'Yes, sir' to the army, and then we sell the red bastards what they want. I don't say as I agree with it, but I don't want the U.S. gov'ment telling me how to mind my business.

"Now you take Olley. Like I says, his pa is a chief, but that don't mean beans to anyone in Yuma. What does mean something is that the old man and a couple of the shakers and movers in that tribe own the Injun ferry down the river, and they do a brisk business. That means lots of dollars passing through his fingers. You know what it costs to cross the river on his boat?"

Mandell had to admit that he did not, and he didn't much care either, but the bartender intended on telling him just the same.

"Four dollars for a wagon and horses, a dollar fifty for a saddle horse, fifty-five cents a head for cattle, thirty cents for sheep. Hell, that old Indian makes as much money on one crossing as I take in all day working this here saloon. And you know where half that money goes?"

"To pay off Olley's bar bill?" Mandell suggested.

"You got that right, mister."

"Isn't there any concern that the Indians will get hostile with all that whiskey available?"

"The Quechans?" He laughed a thunderous rumble that quieted the house again. "Ain't had trouble with them since 1850, when the army bloodied their noses a bit over the murder of a no-good ferry operator named Glanton. But that was before I got here — hell, it was before there was anything here, includin' the railroad."

Mandell figured there still wasn't anything worth mentioning here in Yuma, but kept that to himself. He glanced out the dingy window at the black engine arriving at the Southern Pacific depot and checked his watch. It was somehow comforting that at least something in this corner of hell followed a schedule.

"Want another?"

To Mandell's surprise, he had drained the mug, and to his further surprise, he assented to another.

"The Scotsman here says you're a mining engineer."

"That is correct," Mandell said. Well, it was what he was telling people these days.

The bartender gathered up his and McPeevy's mug and walked back to a barrel to refill them. When he returned he said, "I wouldn't have pegged you for that line of work."

Mandell pushed a coin across the bar. "What line of work would you have pegged me for?"

The bartender snatched up the change and considered him a moment, working his unlovely lips into a knot. "I don't know. I suppose a drummer of some kind."

Mandell laughed. "No, thanks." McPeevy shifted his view from King Robert the Second long enough to allow a grin.

The bartender glanced at McPeevy. "And you're an accountant?"

"Aye, that I am," he said, prodding the unconscious cat.

"And you're both waiting for the boat to take you up the river? Let me guess. The only boat that never leaves on time is Captain Patronoff's *Bad Water*, and the only place the *Bad Water* travels is up to the *Mina del Agua Mala*."

Mandell said, "Pretty fair guessing. Is the place as bad as its name?"

The bartender laughed and shook his head. "Naw." Then he leaned close and his voice lost its banter. "It's worse. You listen to me. Take care. No good ever came out of the Bad Water Mine."

McPeevy frowned and patted his forehead with his stained handkerchief. "Saints! I'll never speak evilly of Kansas City again. Whatever compelled me to accept a position in a place like this?"

"Ain't nothing wrong with this place," the bartender said, and wandered off to other business.

Mandell frowned. What had the bartender meant — or was it only his own suspicious nature that made him read more into that warning than was intended?

4

From the East Bank Saloon down to the river, the mosquitoes closed in around him like a brigade of hungry soldiers. Mandell turned up the collar of his jacket despite the heat, buttoned it tight, and pulled his hat down firmly onto his head. That left only his hands, ears, and cheeks exposed. A defensible position, he mused, swatting the voracious beasts with a sadistic pleasure that would have been foreign to him only four days earlier.

The road took a steep plunge and then he was on the levee where four steam riverboats were moored. These were the bright, orderly, hugely profitable property of the Southern Pacific Company, and they seemed to be a beehive of commercial activity. Downstream, past the pilings and cross members of the Southern Pacific trestle that spanned the Colorado River, were barges tied at their moorings, in various stages of being loaded or offloaded.

Mandell wiped the sweat from his forehead and patted his mustache dry with the sleeve of his coat. He tugged his small-brimmed bowler hat back onto his head, eyeing with a bit of envy the wide, light, airy straw hats that both men and women wore in this country.

The river at this point was a confusion of eddies and currents. Across it was the state of California and a cavalry outpost called Fort Yuma. His eye came back. Not fifty yards out in water was a sandbar that had not been there two days before. He frowned. It was a treacherous river, and if there had been any other convenient way to reach his destination . . .

Mandell turned his feet onto a dusty road that followed the river. A few hundred yards farther up was a rickety, termite-infested assemblage of wood: the exclusive docking place of the riverboat that belonged to the *Mina del Agua Mala* Mining Company. He ventured out onto the pier, avoiding the gaping holes where complete planks were missing, or in otherwise various states of decay. At the tips of his shoes, Mandell had dizzying glimpses of the moving water down below. He stepped carefully, wondering how cargo was loaded without mishaps, and if the lawyers for the mining company were kept busy settling suits.

On a fairly solid section of pier, he stopped to study the riverboat moored there. Her main deck, and the boiler deck above it, had been loaded with mounds of supplies for the trip upriver. The canvas-covered bundles had not been there two days before. That, at least, was an encouraging indication that the boat would be departing soon.

"Hello?" he called, and got back only silence. The gangplank that stretched out to the pier was made of solid stuff. It helped in some small way to bolster Mandell's morale as he put his weight experimentally onto it. On the deck of the riverboat he paused to look for any signs of life.

"Hello? Anyone on board?"

The *Bad Water* was a sturdy little vessel constructed along the lines of an upper Missouri River stern-wheeler. She was about 150 feet long and 40 feet abeam. She carried her weight low, for stability, and drew but twenty inches of water when unloaded. Yet she could shuffle 200 tons of freight up a hazardous, shallow river like the Colorado, skipping easily over submerged sandbars and snags. And when she did run aground, she was equipped with a pair of sturdy wooden spars and a steam-powered capstan to "grasshopper" her over them.

Mandell had to admit that the *Bad Water* was a handsome vessel — in a utilitarian sort of way. He had traveled on larger and fancier riverboats, of course, on the Mississippi, but this little work horse compared favorably.

The Mississippi!

Now, that was a *real* river! Wide, deep, graceful almost in its stately journey from

Minnesota down to the Gulf of Mexico. A real river for real riverboats — the kind that hung their paddles off the side and took deep, powerful bites out of the water, instead of these little Missouri-style stern-wheelers with paddles that only barely dipped the wild waters of lesser rivers. Not that the Mississippi didn't harbor its own dangers. It did, and every one of her pilots would be quick to brag on his own narrow escapes, but at least on the Mississippi there were long, quiet stretches where a man could enjoy the passing shoreline, with a cool drink, and no mosquitoes!

Mandell glanced forward. The boiler was not fired up. Its smokestacks were silent. Long, thin white clouds passed high above them where he had hoped to see the black, billowing smoke that would have signaled an imminent departure. Disappointed, his view moved along the main deck toward the stern of the boat.

From that direction came the sounds of activity and men's voices. He angled across the deck to the port side where he paused by the railing to peer out at the miserable excuse of a river. Aft, by the big, stilled paddle wheel, a handful of bare-backed men were struggling to lift a ponderous wooden beam into place. One man straddled the paddle-wheel support, while another with a huge, leather mallet stood ready by the port-side steam engine. And in between them, four more grunted and strained, muscles bulging, seemingly oblivious to the swarms of black gnats that hovered about them in an ebony fog.

The man with the mallet spied Mandell coming back and immediately dropped the tool and rushed over, smiling hugely, his slant-eyes narrowing even further as he did so. He wore a wide, straw hat — wider than his narrow shoulders — and a long, black braid fell down the back of a muslin shirt that at one time had been bleached white. A pair of gray pantaloons tied at the waist with a rope and straw slippers on his feet completed the outfit.

The man stopped in front of Mandell and bowed deeply three times and said, "Ah, Mr. Manderr. So good to see you again."

"Hello, Chan." He nodded his head at the work going on by the paddle wheel. "I was hoping you'd be about ready to get under way today."

Chan Loo showed glistening, white teeth. "No can leave yet, Mr. Manderr. Connecting rod crackee almost in two. Had to makee new again. Veddy, veddy bad to go upriver with crack in connecting rod. Veddy, veddy dangerous."

Mandell frowned. "Is the captain around?"

Chan pointed up at the deck overhead where the main cabin was located — the boiler deck as it was called, although Mandell never could understand why since the boiler sat down on the main deck. "Captain up in gentl'man's card room." He prodded the air a couple more times with his finger and smiled.

"The gentleman's card room?" Mandell had heard of such things on the Mississippi River. The card room was actually a part of the main cabin closed off with a curtain when meals were not being served, but it surprised him that this little boat, on a river like the Colorado, would have anything equivalent. "I will go up and talk to him."

"Captain already have guest. A veddy, veddy pretty guest."

"Oh?"

Chan was nodding his head. "Lady passenger. Only just arrivee. Up in gentl'man's card room." He clucked disapprovingly. "Mr. Manderr? You wantee somethin' cold to drink?"

Mandell came to a stop and turned back. "You have something cold to drink?" His voice held more than just a hint of surprise.

"Yes, yes. Tea." Chan reached over the railing and hauled a cord up out of the water with a sealed mason jar tied to the end. "You go up now, Mr. Manderr. I have the missus bringee up to you in two shakes!"

Mandell grinned at Chan's ingenious cooling system, and thought that the bartender down at the East Bank Saloon could take a lesson or two from the clever Chinese boat mechanic and handyman.

5

He knocked on the door to the main cabin.

"What do you want?" came a curt reply.

Mandell reached for the knob and heard heavy footsteps thump on the floor beyond. The door slammed open and a bearded face put itself in his way, puffing furiously at a foul-smelling cigar.

Captain Alexis Patronoff was a few inches shorter than Mandell, but massively built — like a bear. And like a bear, his face was buried in a forest of hair. His hands were giant paws — with black hair curling about the knuckles. They gripped the door jamb, and Mandell imagined them able to rip the wood out in chunks. Patronoff's eyes might have been black, though Mandell suspected they were a dark shade of brown, and that their deep sockets and the bony brow ridges only made them appear like an angry night storm. The captain wore a dark-blue billed cap with gold braid. The last time Mandell had spoken with Patronoff he had worn a heavy, blue sea captain's coat. Today, in deference to the heat, he was in shirt sleeves sans the collar, and his dark-gray suspenders followed the bulging curve of his belly up over the mountainous terrain of his shoulders.

In contrast to the rough appearance, Patronoff's teeth, although flecked with fragments of tobacco, had been scrubbed white as if with baking soda, and his fingernails were carefully trimmed and filed — each the exact same length, without a hint of ship's grime beneath.

Patronoff paused in the open doorway and a small change reshaped his impatient face. "Oh. It's only you, Mandell," he said as if he had expected someone else. Just the same, he did not seem happy seeing him standing there.

"Captain," Mandell said briefly.

Patronoff wheeled away without another word and returned to the table where the woman was sitting. He eased his bulk into a chair that seemed too small for him. "Well, don't just stand there, man, come in."

Mandell removed his hat. If the heat outside was oppressive, the conditions in the cabin were enough to smother a man. The cabin was a long, narrow room, and every window in the place was shut up tight. White curtains covered the view to the outside, and that was fine with him. As far as the detective was concerned, there wasn't a whole lot worth looking at beyond them.

There was a liquor cabinet and a bar

against the wall by the door, and in the middle of the floor was the long table with eight chairs on each side and a chair on each end. The captain and the lady sat across from each other at the nearer end of the table, and it was suddenly clear why the captain should be annoyed at the interruption.

She had striking eyes, wide and brown. They watched him with intelligence. She had bearing, and the poise that came with several years attending finishing school, Mandell was certain. Her brown hair was pulled up on top of her head and hidden within the confines of a wide, beige hat. She wore a dark-gray skirt and matching jacket over a white blouse fastened at the neck with a brooch. She sat straight in the chair — perfect finishing school posture — her hands clasped on the table near a handbag. A carpetbag resided on the floor by her chair.

Mandell noted other details too, ones not so obvious, as he came across the room.

Captain Patronoff narrowed an eye at him and said with a suddenness, "Blast it, man! Close that door before you let in every damn mosquito on the river!" He glanced at the woman. "Pardon, ma'am."

Mandell swung it closed, stifling even the faintest of breezes that might have tempered the oven that he found himself in. Patronoff puffed frantically at his cigar and swatted his neck.

"Blasted beasts! They'll eat you alive if you let them."

The woman gave Mandell a scrutinizing look, as if trying to determine just what sort of man he was. From his clothing, he could have filled many roles, and that was the point of it. In the end, she'd just have to keep guessing. She licked the beads of moisture from her upper lip and patted her forehead with a white handkerchief. Mandell smiled in a way he hoped would put her at ease. He surmised that she was traveling alone and, as such, might be apprehensive for her safety after being deposited, as he had been, in this wild southwestern town.

Remembering proper etiquette — at least what passed for proper etiquette as far as the captain was concerned — Patronoff waved his cigar in his general direction and said, "This here is Harrison Mandell, Miss Haven. He's one of the passengers, and there will be a few others." Then he reversed the introductions. "Mandell, Miss Rose Haven. She's going upriver with us."

Rose Haven smiled at him. He bowed slightly, his hat clasped in both hands. Even in the wilting heat, she was by far the loveliest woman he'd seen anywhere in this part of the country. She would have been stunning dressed for dinner, the very jewel of any party in Chicago, or Boston.

"How very nice to make your acquaintance, Miss Haven," he said, and out the corner of his eye saw the scowl come to Patronoff's face.

He held Rose's eye for a moment longer than absolutely necessary, then directed his attention to the captain. "I apologize for the interruption."

Patronoff grunted and waved his cigar in the air, indicating that it was of no consequence — unconvincingly.

"I was wondering about your schedule. We were supposed to leave for the mine two days ago."

"Delays, Mr. Mandell. They happen all the time. Them up at the mine, they expect them. I'll get you there when I can. No keeping anything as civilized as a schedule on this god—" He glanced at Rose. "Pardon again, ma'am. This miserable excuse of a river."

"Do you have an idea how much longer? Another day? Perhaps two?"

Patronoff swatted a mosquito and puffed a cloud of smoke into the trapped heat of the cabin. Rose coughed quietly into her hand. It went unnoticed by the captain.

"We're replacing a damaged connecting rod at this very moment, Mandell. The job should be completed by evening. If everything goes without a hitch, we can be getting up a head of steam tomorrow noon. Don't worry. You'll know when. I'll give five pulls on the whistle when I'm ready to have you aboard."

Concern came to Rose's eyes. "But, Captain, what shall I do until then? I was not informed that there might be a delay in getting to *Mina del Agua Mala*."

Patronoff gave a short laugh. "There is probably a lot of things you weren't told, ma'am. The truth of the matter is, the mine owners haven't had much luck keeping school teachers around. It's a rough place, ma'am. The men are a hard lot, and their women are too. Have to be to live out in a hellhole — pardon again — like the Bad Water Mine. It only stands to reason their kids are a hard lot too."

Rose looked concerned.

Mandell said, "You are just off the train that pulled in earlier?"

"Why, yes, I am. How did you know that, Mr. Mandell?"

He smiled easily and said, "I have been trapped in this place for four days now, and I am certain I have seen every face in town. But I have not seen yours. I would have remembered. Beyond that, there is a Southern Pacific baggage ticket stub still on your bag."

"How very clever of you."

Patronoff grunted and was about to say something when a knock at the door snapped his hairy head around. "Go away!"

The door opened and a small face looked

in. "Don't tell me to go away, Captain Patronoff. I go away and you not eat this entire trip. Cold drinks?" A small woman in a white dress and a wide red sash shuffled in and closed the door behind her.

"Yes, please," Rose said at once, as if she feared the offer might be withdrawn if not pounced upon immediately.

Patronoff nodded his head. "Sorry. Bring the refreshments in, Loo Han Ling."

The Chinese woman bowed quickly and brought over the tray bearing three glasses, filled with a dark liquid, with beads of moisture forming on their outsides. And it was cold!

Mandell drank his down, relishing the temperature, if not the tea itself. Tea had never been his favorite drink. He liked his beverages a bit stouter, but at the moment, anything cold was welcome.

The captain tipped up his glass and drained it, and for a fleeting moment allowed a smile to settle upon his face.

"This is very good," Rose said, sipping in a proper fashion, though Mandell suspected she wanted to guzzle like the rest of them.

Finishing school, he mused. All women should be required to attend — and some men too, he decided, watching Patronoff slouch down into his chair.

Loo Han Ling seemed satisfied and left them there, once again shutting out any chance of a breeze as she disappeared into the blazing afternoon. The captain came out of his slouch and belched — and pardoned himself.

"Ought to be grateful for the delay, Miss Haven. If it weren't for it, we'd have left two days ago, and you'd be stuck in Yuma until I made the return trip, and that might be two, three weeks."

"Then I suppose I ought to be grateful," she said, but she didn't sound happy about the situation. She looked at Mandell, her curiosity needing to be satisfied, and asked, "You are employed at the mine, sir?"

"I am a mining engineer, Miss Haven," the detective lied. "Like you, this will be my first trip."

"Oh. Then you must have been hired through the post. On the basis of your credentials?"

"I have a degree."

"You were trained in Europe, then. At Freiberg? Or perhaps *École des Mines* in Paris?"

Mandell grinned and evaded the question with "You have a wide knowledge of mining engineering, ma'am. Quite impressive."

She smiled. "I am a teacher. It is my business to keep well informed."

"Then I shall look forward to speaking further with you. The trip, I understand, will take several days. We will have time to talk later. I . . . er, I ought to be going now."

Rose said, "Is there a hotel in Yuma where I can get a room?"

"The Southern Pacific Hotel is nearby. I have taken a room there myself."

"I will walk with you, then." She glanced at the captain. "My luggage is at the depot. Is there someone who can transport it to the boat, Captain Patronoff?"

"I'll send a man 'round for it this afternoon."

"Thank you." She took her handbag from the table and stood. Mandell lifted her carpetbag. She gave him a smile for which he would have gladly carried a dozen stuffed carpetbags.

The captain remained seated, glowering at the tip of the cigar in his fingers.

All at once the report of a gun boomed outside the windows. Patronoff scowled and came out of his chair. Mandell set the carpetbag on the floor as Patronoff threw back the curtain and heaved up the sash.

On the dock below was a man in a wide hat, a short red jacket over a bright-yellow shirt, open upon his dark, sweaty neck, and black striped pants with — what Mandell thought — were big silver buttons down the side. His feet were clad in tall, black leather boots, their high heels bedecked with shiny big-roweled spurs. At his waist was the butt of a revolver, facing forward, and across his chest was a bandolier of ammunition. At the moment the man was breaking open the breech of a Springfield rifle and inserting a fresh cartridge into the chamber.

"What the devil, man!" Patronoff bellowed.

His sudden grin made a huge mustache hitch up, and he said, "Someone is home after all, no? I am looking for the captain. I am told his name is Patronoff."

"I am Captain Patronoff. What is so blasted important that you have to take pot shots at my boat?"

"I no shoot the boat." He laughed. "The air. I shoot in the air. I called out. No one hears." The man shrugged his shoulders.

Mandell glanced down the dock where two other men waited on the bank, holding the reins to three horses, weighted down with so much armament that if they were to fall into the river they'd sink immediately to the bottom like an anchor — and stay there.

"Well, you have my attention now. What is it you want?"

"Passage, *Señor* Captain. Up the *río*. It is said in Yuma Town that you will be making the trip soon."

"This is a freighter. There are other boats that will carry you upriver."

The man glanced at his friends on the river bank then back. "*Sí*, but they not leave so soon as your boat. We have money to pay," he said.

"I'll just bet you do," Patronoff grunted under his breath. Louder, he said, "Sorry. This ain't a packet you can book passage on. We don't carry passengers, except those in the employ of the *Mina del Agua Mala,* or thems with other legitimate business. You got business at the Bad Water Mine? No business, no family, no friends at the Bad Water, no ride on my boat."

The Mexican glanced at his friends, then a sly grin crept across his face. "The mine, it is where we must go, *Señor* Captain. You must take us."

Patronoff narrowed an eye. "What is your business there?"

The Mexican put his hands on his waist, grinning. In a grand gesture he indicated his partners waiting along the bank, he said, "My *amigos* and me, we are, how do you say, *cocineros.*"

Rose moved up to Mandell's side and said softly, "He is saying that he and his friends are cooks."

"Cooks?" Patronoff looked at her skeptically.

Below, the Mexican was saying "We make *muy* fine *enchiladas* and *empanadas de carne* for the *hombres* that dig the silver, no?" He grinned.

Patronoff made a dubious frown, but he said, "Just make sure you're ready to leave when I am. I'll give five pulls on my whistle when we are ready. One more thing, no horses. Agreed?"

"*Sí*, we will be ready. Ah, *Señor* Captain, when do you leave?"

"Maybe tomorrow, maybe the next day. We leave when I'm ready."

"You cannot maybe leave sooner?"

"I said we leave when I'm ready, and not a minute before. Good day to you." Patronoff shut the window and looked at Mandell. "That's all we need, the likes of them on board."

"Who are they?"

"I've seen their kind plenty of times. Riff-raff. Up from Mexico. Probably chased over the border by their own government. Trouble, plain and simple. Don't want 'em on my boat, but if they got business up at the mine I'm obliged to give them passage."

"Do you believe them?" Rose asked.

Patronoff said, "I've heard of stranger things, but it ain't my job to ferret out the truth. The mine don't give me a manifest of them who they are expectin'."

Mandell hefted Rose's luggage again and shifted his view back to Patronoff. "Well, let's hope for a tomorrow departure, then."

"You'll hear my whistle when we're ready," Patronoff said, pulling open the door.

The air outside was almost pleasant compared to the main cabin, although immediately the mosquitoes attacked from all sides like wild Apaches. Rose stepped ahead of Mandell through the narrow canyon of canvas-covered mounds. As she started down the stairs she moved to the right for the man who had started up from the main deck. He was a tall, lean fellow with a magnificent mustache and a sunburned face beneath a wide hat. He wore a brown vest, tall-heeled boots, and a Colt revolver at his hip. He gave Rose a pleasant smile as he passed. Gave Mandell the briefest of nods without the smile.

He ascended the steps and went to the main cabin. Mandell glanced back in time to see Patronoff's swarthy face blanch as the man approached him. Rose noted the captain's curious reaction too and looked back questioningly at the Pinkerton detective.

6

"What do you think that was all about?" she asked as she lifted her skirts to negotiate the gangplank.

Mandell followed Rose down to the rickety pier. "Watch your step here," he advised as she alighted on the precarious contrivance that he suspected one day soon must topple into the river. Then: "I don't know. Captain Patronoff seemed quite put off by my appearance, as if he thought I was someone else."

"That man with the big revolver?"

"Perhaps."

"I hope it doesn't mean trouble."

Mandell gave a short laugh. "It wouldn't surprise me. Seems that everything that can go wrong has gone wrong. Watch yourself there. Here, let me help you." He took her arm and guided her around a missing plank. "There you go."

"Thank you. It's nearly impossible to see some of them."

"It's your skirts. They obstruct your view. And this dock is not quite up to the casual stroll, Miss Haven."

"It *was* almost as if he were expecting that

man. Did you have that impression?"

"Here we go. Terra firma at last." Mandell turned back to look at the riverboat moored to the uncertain structure they had just surmounted.

"I mean, well, after all," she went on, starting on the road, "he was quite brusque when you knocked, almost as if he were anticipating something."

Mandell grinned. "I think that Captain Patronoff would have been unhappy with any interruption just at the moment."

She looked at him, a little confused at first, then gave him a smirk when she caught his meaning. "I'm certain his intentions weren't anything but honorable."

"No doubt."

They walked toward town and the Southern Pacific Hotel. An imposing structure for a place like Yuma — two stories high with covered porches running around it on both levels.

Mandell discovered he was smiling. In Rose Haven's company the heat of the land was somehow abated, the landscape was not quite so bleak, and the swarms of mosquitoes didn't follow him as closely — and they didn't seem to accost Rose at all — or at the very least, she refrained from swatting them with the gusto and sheer pleasure he had recently developed.

"The hotel appears civilized enough," Rose

said, halting in front of it and looking the place over as if trying to decide whether to stay there or continue on to the next place. The detective was about to tell her the next place would certainly be a step down from the Southern Pacific Hotel, decided instead to simply advise her these accommodations were a new addition to Yuma, having been built shortly after the railroad came through in 1877. The hotel was a scant seven years old, a mere babe when measured against some of the local hovels dating back to around 1779.

"Well, at least it is close to the river," she said, tugging resolutely at the purse strap over her shoulder as if coming to a decision.

Mandell followed her up the stairs, hauling the carpetbag along. Inside the lobby Rose arranged for a room at the desk while Mandell admired the construction of the hotel. Its open covered porches effectively shaded the inside against the unrelenting sun and at the same time allowed a breeze to move constantly through the building. It had been well designed, eminently suited for the climate. His own room was located on the second floor, facing the river. With door and window open, the days had been barely tolerable and the nights almost pleasant.

Rose came across the lobby with a brass key in her hand and a smile that made him forget the heat. "I'm all set for the night, Mr.

Mandell. Thank you for your recommendation, and your aid." She hefted her bag, signaling the end to her need of his help and that she intended to proceed to her room alone.

"My pleasure, Miss Haven. Perhaps I'll see you again?"

"No doubt. We will be traveling upriver together."

He smiled and said, "I was hoping that perhaps before then. The hotel has an excellent dining room. Would you care to join me for dinner this evening?"

His invitation seemed to catch her off guard. Uncertainty showed on her face, and he wondered if perhaps he wasn't rushing things. She recovered at once though, and said, "I will be happy to join you at dinner, Mr. Mandell."

"Seven o'clock?"

"Seven o'clock will be fine. It will give me time to rest up after my trip."

"It helps to leave the door open," he said. "These rooms are ovens otherwise. The doors have a hold-open chain so apparently the idea of cross ventilation was in the design."

She graced him with one of her lovely smiles again. "Thank you. I'll do that."

As she walked away he called after her, "I'll see you at seven," and a moment later he found himself back outside on the dusty road, with no recollection at all of leaving the hotel or descending the steps. He started into Yuma, remembered something and wheeled back, taking the outside stairs up to the second floor where his room was located. Inside, he retrieved a book from his luggage, shoved it under his arm, grinned at himself in a mirror, and rubbed the stubble of a beard with his fingers. He put a shave and a bath next on his agenda and went back outside.

King Robert the Second lay curled up in the valise by the corner, his head propped up on the edge looking out, an unhealthy glaze to his green eyes, Mandell thought, when he dropped his book onto the table and pulled back a chair. Gilligan McPeevy came awake with a start and almost toppled over backward in his chair.

"Saints!" He yawned and rubbed his eyes. "What time is it?" he asked even as he was pulling his watch from his vest pocket. He groaned, mumbled some complaint about it being still early, and pushed the watch back. "Where did you get off to?"

"I was down at the docks, checking on our transportation up the river."

McPeevy's eyes fluttered closed, sleepily. "And?"

"And it looks like we are stuck here at least another day. Captain Patronoff says the chances are good we can leave tomorrow."

"That sly Greek has been saying that since we arrived." McPeevy opened one eye and directed it at Mandell. "What's that you are reading?"

He held the book's spine up toward him.

McPeevy leaned forward, opening the other eye. "*Fulbright's Source Book on Mining Engineering?*" He hitched up a questioning brow.

"Just brushing up."

"Hmmm. On what? Mining in the devil's own back yard?"

"Schools."

"Schools?" McPeevy yawned again and slouched back in the chair. "Ye know, Harry, I was a thinkin' that ye might have been right when ye suggested the other day that we rent a couple horses. Gracious. By this time we'd have easily ridden to the mine."

"And you were correct in pointing out that there is hostile country between here and the *Mina del Agua Mala,* and perhaps hostile Indians too." The detective caught the bartender's attention and raised two fingers. "Besides, from what I understand there is not a patch a shade within a hundred miles of Yuma."

McPeevy chuckled, his eyes closed. "Aye, there is something to be said for a cozy pub if waiting is all ye can do." Suddenly he sniffed the air. Then sniffed again and followed his nose forward. "What is that I am smelling?" he asked suspiciously, and looked at Mandell. "It's coming from ye."

Mandell shut the book. "It's called a bath and shave."

"It's called toilet water!"

"It's called Bombay Mint."

"Why on earth, man?"

"I have a dinner date."

"A dinner date? With a woman?" McPeevy narrowed an eye at Mandell. "Not that fiery redhead wench we saw earlier?"

Mandell laughed. "Yes, it is with a woman, and no, it is not that one."

"Where did ye find a female in this place?"

"There are plenty of women around."

"Sure, man, if ye don't mind 'em brown as nuts with skin like shoe leather."

"This lady is not a native of Yuma, and her skin has not been ravaged by the local conditions. She is just off the train from San Diego, and she will be traveling with us upriver."

"To the *Mina del Agua Mala?*"

"She's a schoolteacher."

"Saints! What would prompt a woman of culture to come to a place like this?"

"Children that need to be educated, I should think. A most admirable calling."

McPeevy grunted.

The beers arrived, warm as usual. McPeevy

sipped his drink and asked after a moment, "Is she a good-looking woman?"

Mandell didn't answer that — he didn't need to. The grin that came to his face said all that needed saying.

7

The King yowled.

A terrified, ear-piercing, nerve-grating cry of pain and fright that instantly drew the attention of every man in the place.

Gilligan McPeevy came out of his nap with a start, choked back half a snore, and threw a panicky look around the saloon . . . and then down at the corner.

The valise was empty.

Mandell put down his book and looked over.

By the bar a man had leaped straight up into the air, and if he could have flown, Mandell figured he would have headed directly for the coal oil lamp fixture on the ceiling a dozen feet overhead and latched onto it.

He was a slender man, long of arm and leg, with a bushy mustache that covered his upper lip. He wore a wide hat in the style of a Texas cowboy, and brown boots with his black pants stuffed in all around their tops. On his chest was a brown wool vest buttoned over a dingy, faded red shirt with its sleeves rolled up, and on his hip there was a long-barrel Colt revolver.

Mandell noted these details in a glance, and it occurred to him suddenly that he had seen this man before. Then he remembered where — on the stairs of the *Bad Water* as Rose Haven and he had been leaving. The very man who had caused Captain Patronoff to blanch at the sight of him.

The man landed from his flight to the ceiling, tottering on the high heels of his boots trying to keep afoot, and at the same time roared, "What the hell!" His eyes narrowed at the source of the hair-raising cry, and in a movement that gave no warning, he took aim with the tip of his pointy boot and sent King Robert the Second reeling along the floor.

The cat dug in his claws, bringing himself to a drifting halt, eyed the oncoming cowboy, and sprang into the air, landing with a thump on Gilligan's lap. Immediately he proceeded to claw his way under the Scotsman's vest.

"There, there, my darlin'," McPeevy cried, himself in half a frenzy endeavoring to extract the crazed feline from the folds of his shirt. He winced, gritted his teeth, and tugged, but the cat's claws were securely locked into the material of his clothing. The King yowled pitifully.

With determined strides, the tall cowboy was on his way over. Mandell could see nothing but revenge blazing in the man's hard eyes.

"I nearly busted my leg over that damned cat," the cowboy was growling. "That no-good animal has seen the last foot he's gonna ever get under!"

It was apparent that this irate fellow had no idea King Robert the Second belonged to McPeevy, only that it had wound up on his lap. It was also apparent that the lanky outdoorsman had a healthy disregard for cats, and intended to vent his wrath on the unfortunate animal whose only crime was to have inadvertently put its tail in the path of this fellow's heavy boot.

The cowboy grabbed up King Robert the Second by the scruff of its neck, and Mandell didn't know who was more surprised, McPeevy or the King himself.

"Say here . . ." Gilligan started to protest.

But the cowboy wasn't listening. He flung the cat toward the ceiling. As it tumbled head over paws, the man reached down for the revolver at his waist and pulled the long weapon out, cocking back the hammer as it came free of the leather. Men all around the saloon who had been chuckling an instant before suddenly dove for cover when he took aim.

The revolver roared. For a moment the sound of it deafened the barroom. Then King Robert the Second came down screaming a blood-curdling yowl. Claws bared, the cat hit the floor running, and in a blink of an eye was gone beneath the swinging doors.

In an instant the cowboy realized he had missed his shot, and a second or two later he discovered why.

His rage shifted from the long-departed cat. A quiet came over the room as he looked Mandell in the eyes and then at his arm locked in the vise-grip that had knocked aside his aim.

The two men considered each other.

Mandell lowered his voice so that only this man could hear. It was a friendly, almost soothing voice, but there was a cold edge of menace in it that was undeniable. "Cats are mighty poor fare, sir. Would you care to try that on someone more your own size?" Beneath his grip, Mandell felt hard muscle. This would not be an easy man to put down if he allowed him the privilege of the first blow. He heard Gilligan McPeevy scrambling out of his chair and caught sight of a figure darting for the batwing doors. Then McPeevy was gone, and the barroom held its collective breath.

The cowboy spoke through clenched teeth, his words measured and even spaced, as if the rage within him only permitted speech in compact units. "You don't know what trouble you're in for, mister."

Mandell allowed an easy grin to move across his face. "Perhaps not. But I don't recommend that you attempt to show me."

The cowboy's vision seemed to clear then, and he got a handle on his anger. His gray eyes spent a moment taking in this man who had come between him and his pleasure. The Pinkerton man knew what he was seeing, and what that would be telling him. A tall man, more wiry than husky, dressed in civilized clothes. A cosmopolitan man, perhaps. More at home among city streets and friendly office buildings than in the harsh wilderness of this place? A man as tamed as his environment . . . perhaps? Mandell grinned wryly to himself. But clothes often lie, and a Chicago back alley is hardly civilized by any standards.

He eased off on the cowboy's wrist, but not his guard, which remained at a hair-trigger setting. The place to watch was the eyes. The eyes always gave a man away — unless the man was very, very good. Mandell saw them narrow as he released his grip, but he didn't see the signs of an immediate attack.

The man wrenched his hand free and, still holding the revolver, put a step of distance between them. But this lanky gent in the wide hat would not use the weapon. He didn't have to. There was enough muscle in him for his fists and knees to do whatever he felt needed doing.

The man grinned then and said in a voice

almost congenial, "You're lucky I'm in a generous mood, mister. You might have been in big difficulty otherwise." He shoved the revolver into his holster and turned back toward the bar.

Mandell lost sight of his eyes, and the warning that sounded in his brain was like the shift-change whistle at a Colorado coal mine. There were the other signals too: the tenseness that stretched his vest across his back, the bunching of his shoulders, the pivot and solid planting of his right foot as he turned away. Mandell had seen them all before, and each time they had forewarned the same thing.

Mandell slipped his hand into the pocket of his jacket for the knuckle dusters he carried there, then changed his mind. When this fellow attacked, it was going to be with fists, and brawn, and Mandell would meet him on his own terms.

"I'd think twice," he said barely above a whisper. A part of him wanted to avoid what he knew was coming; he'd just bathed, and had only one good suit with him, and he didn't particularly want to deal with this in the heat and river humidity of this place. But Yuma had gotten under his skin like an irritant, and another part of him itched to have a go around.

The man heard the low-spoken warning, looked over his shoulder, and grinned. He turned back toward the bar, then without warning wheeled around, knuckles curled into a hard knot. He had calculated exactly where Mandell stood, had struck out unerringly for the point where his jaw should have been.

And, as with the cat, he missed.

The detective ducked as the arm arced overhead. He took aim at a target that was bigger than the point of a man's chin. Big targets are easier to hit, and this one would be exposed, not expecting attack. With driving force, Mandell hit the cowboy below the rib cage. No soft flesh here. Hard muscle, like the steel bands of an oaken pickle barrel. He had anticipated that. Hard muscle was the preferred target — it didn't absorb the shock as easily as flab did.

The jarring blow sent a wave of pain up his arm, but he ignored it. The cowboy bent in half, as if hinged in the middle. Mandell repeated the punch, his fist glancing off the buckle of the man's holster belt this time.

This cowboy was no green willow out for a night of fun. He had seen the business end of a fist a time or two. The fellow reeled away and snatched up a chair. Curiously, he seemed to be having a bit of trouble breathing, as if suddenly he wasn't pulling in enough air, but that wasn't going to stop him.

"You know any prayers, I recommend you start saying them now," the cowboy said, gasping.

The prattle was only an excuse to catch his breath. The detective jogged left and the chair shattered upon the table immediately behind where he had been standing. The cowboy looked surprised, as if he expected to see Mandell somewhere beneath the rubble.

The surprise vanished. Mandell materialized from another direction and planted a right hook to his chin. The cowboy staggered, his chin open to the bone and red dripping to his shirt.

He came back swinging, but his feet were suddenly unsteady, and those high heels didn't help matters much either. His breathing was louder now, like he was choking on a peach pit.

"I do know a prayer," Mandell said, hammering in a salvo of short, fast punches. "It starts *'Now I lay you down to sleep. . . .'*" He hit him again, low, and followed it with a left jab that snapped his head back.

The cowboy's gray eyes glazed, yet there was still fight left in them. Mandell moved in close with a volley of body punches dished out with a prizefighter's speed and precision.

" *'And pray the Lord your fists don't meet.'* "

The cowboy was buckling.

Mandell caught him by the front of his shirt, felt something hard and sharp beneath his hand. He hauled back. The blow staggered the tall cowboy, sent him backpedaling over the bar with a crash of glassware. He landed in a heap at the bartender's feet, tried to raise himself, fell back into the puddle of beer dripping from a spilled mug on the bar, and there he remained.

"Amen," Mandell gasped.

He straightened up a chair and sat down, drawing breath like fire into his lungs. The men around him began to move again. There were appreciative slaps on the back and words of praise. At the bartender's bidding, two men picked up the cowboy and heaved him out into the street.

"That was beautiful," the bartender said, bringing a beer to his table. His ugly mug twisted into something resembling a smile.

"Thanks," Mandell said, suddenly looking forward to the flat beer. Thinking it over, he was amazed that the cowboy hadn't touched him once. The fight could have gone in a decidedly different direction if he had allowed the man's bony knuckles to connect. He discovered he was still holding a piece of the man's shirt in his left hand — the piece with something hard in it.

As he opened his hand the late-afternoon sunlight glinted on a six-pointed star of dull nickel; bold letters engraved into it:

DEPUTY U.S. MARSHAL.

8

"You've hurt your hand," she said, reaching across the white tablecloth to take it gently in her soft fingers.

Mandell grinned depreciatingly at the reddened knuckles. "It's nothing. Must have scraped them on something this afternoon." He didn't particularly care to discuss the fight or the bruised fist now. All he wanted to do was study Rose Haven's deep-brown eyes and listen to the music of her voice.

"But shouldn't you put a bandage on it?"

"The air will help it heal."

Rose was a delightful vision for a man who had seen nothing but sand and cactus and the slow waters of the Colorado River forever moving through a desolate country, carrying the red silt of the land down to the ocean. When she had met him in the foyer a few minutes earlier, she had nearly stolen his breath. She was wearing a green silk dress that at first glance seemed to have been comprised of at least a half-dozen layers of lace, ruffles, and pleats — and a bustle! How civilized, and very fashionable . . . for any place but Yuma, Arizona. To see her here in this forsaken land was most refreshing. Over the dress she wore a gray basque, and upon her brown hair, which was rolled into a discreet bun at the back of her head and held in place with ivory pins, was a black velvet hat decorated with silk flowers. The tips of her fingers, protruding from black silk mitts, clutched a black and red velvet purse.

Mandell studiously tried not to stare as he escorted her to the dining room, and as the waiter in his white coat guided them to their table, he couldn't help but feel a twinge of regret that all this lovely finery would be consigned to the bottom of a trunk once they were deposited upon shores of the bleak outpost that he knew the *Mina del Agua Mala* mining town to be.

She frowned at the battle scars and said, "I do hope it does not become infected. Tetanus is such a frightening disease."

He grinned. "It will be all right."

The waiter came by and they ordered dolphin — brought up the Colorado River from the Gulf of California, the waiter informed them — and white wine from Napa Valley vineyards. With the menus removed, Rose folded her hands upon the red napkin and smiled at him. She glanced out the tall windows at the darkening landscape beyond the porch railing and said, "At least it cools down in the evenings. I declare, Mr. Mandell, this place is most unpleasant, although I suppose one would adapt to it over time."

The bottle of wine came in a silver bucket, and it was cold — well, it was colder than air temperature. Apparently the hotel knew something of Chan Loo's trick as well. The waiter filled their goblets and left.

Mandell tasted the zinfandel. "This is not a place I would care to have to adapt to, Miss Haven."

"But you are yourself going to the *Mina del Agua Mala*. Are you not? You did say you were a mining engineer?"

"Yes, certainly. But my position with the mining firm is only temporary — as a consultant, you see." Curious. A twinge of guilt stabbed his conscience when he spoke the lie that in the past had rolled so easily off his tongue. "The fact is, I visit many mines around the country. My — er — company is based in Chicago."

"Oh. I see."

He detected a note of disappointment. Another twinge stabbed him. She glanced down at her wine and sampled it experimentally.

"Mmmm. That's very nice," she said, replacing the goblet. "How long do you expect to remain at the mine, Mr. Mandell?"

"A few months, I should think."

She seemed to brighten at that, and her eyes widened. "Mining has always been an interest of mine. I suppose that is the reason I agreed to accept a teaching position that would take me into this savage land. My mother and father were against it, of course. My brother was concerned for my safety. And perhaps I ought to have been too. All that I read in anticipation did not fully prepare me for the heat and desolation of the trip. And then stepping off that train this afternoon — well, it was like stepping onto another planet."

That was an odd comparison. He had never given planets much thought — except for the one that he found himself living upon: a stage upon which he acted out the fiction of his life.

"I've made a study of mining; it's sort of an avocation of mine, and once I knew I'd be teaching in a mining town I reread every book I could find." She laughed, the sound almost musical.

Whoa, boy. Time to get your head down out of the clouds.

"If I had been a man, I imagine I would have been a mining engineer. Think how much you can learn traveling around the country — the world even."

"It's not all it's cracked up to be, Miss Haven," he said, smiling. "Mostly you just find yourself away from home a lot."

"Where is your home, Mr. Mandell?"

He made a wry face. "How far back do you want me to go? I was born in Colorado. My parents were from Ohio. My father was bitten by the gold bug and swept along in the great rush to California in 'forty-nine, but he never made it any farther than Boulder, Colorado. I'm not often in the state these days. I have a post office box in Chicago, but I'm sometimes away for months and mail backs up on a regular fashion."

"You have any family, Mr. Mandell?" she asked, aligning her knife and forks next to the napkin and crystal water glass as if distracted.

"My mother moved back to Ohio after my father died. I had an older brother. He fell at Missionary Ridge during the war. No one else. And you?"

"Oh, the usual. Mother, father, brother, two sisters, six-soon-to-be-seven cousins, and an assorted menagerie of cats and dogs — the number of them fluctuates almost weekly. They all live in San Francisco or Sacramento."

"And you are the first to break out on your own?"

She looked around the dining room as if viewing the whole world. "I've always been a bit of a venturer. I'm the only one who has ever graduated from college, although my father insisted that each one of his daughters attend Miss Filvia's School of Social Acceptability."

"Sensible father."

She smiled. "And where was it you said

you had graduated from?"

"The Colorado School of Mines," he answered at once.

"Really? I would have thought you from an European school. You seem to be a man with more of a cultured training."

Mandell couldn't help smiling, and it was apparent that Rose immediately regretted her choice of words. Her cheeks flushed, and she averted her eyes, contemplating the folds of her napkin.

"The Colorado School of Mines has a fine reputation. It was established in 1874 as part of the Episcopal University," he said, repeating the information he had gleaned from *Fulbright's* a few hours earlier. "And as for culture, well, Denver has become quite a metropolis in the Rockies. They have concerts, museums, and even an opera company."

"I'm sorry, Mr. Mandell. I have overstepped myself. Certainly I didn't mean . . ."

"No offense taken, Miss Haven." He smiled amiably and hoped this topic would be a closed door for the rest of the trip. It was time to change subjects. "Earlier you seemed to understand what that gentleman down on the dock was saying. Do you speak Spanish?"

"Oh, yes. Quite fluently really. I suppose it was that part of my credentials that persuaded the owners of the *Mina del Agua Mala* to offer me the position. They wanted someone who could freely communicate with the Spanish workers. Some cannot speak English at all, and therefore, neither can their children." She was suddenly abashed flaunting her talents, and she smiled charmingly. "But it is really nothing, I'm sure. Lots of people speak more than one language."

"But it *is* something, Miss Haven. I have difficulty with the one I was born into."

She laughed and he grinned. A movement at the dining-room door caught his eye. Across the room the three women entered. The redhead seemed quite recovered from her earlier fright — perhaps overly so. When the waiter came to seat them she stepped crookedly on her shoe heel, and giggled.

The older woman caught her by the elbow, said something close to her ear, and helped her along to the table. The third woman followed a few steps behind as if embarrassed by it all and immediately buried her face in a menu.

"Do you know them?"

"Huh?"

"You look as if you know those women," Rose said a little stiffly.

"Oh. I didn't realize I was staring," he replied, returning his attention to her.

"I wouldn't have exactly called it staring, Mr. Mandell. It was more like a careful study, as if they were the wing of a fly beneath the lens of a microscope. It was the same look you gave that man down on the dock this afternoon and, in a less obvious manner, the way you looked at me when we first met on the boat." She smiled a most disarming smile. "Do you always analyze people so?"

He mirrored her smile and tasted his wine. "I will try to be more discreet in the future. And, no, I do not know those women, although I have recently seen the one with the outstanding hair — er — out and about town."

Rose looked at him as if wondering if his words held another meaning beyond the obvious. She directed her attention to the woman in question and said, "She is not the sort I would care to discover my brother associated with. Or any honorable man." She looked back at Mandell. "You know what she is, don't you?"

"Yes, ma'am. She is drunk."

Their dinner arrived before Rose could go further. It was a most civilized meal served on bone china. The coffee came in delicate cups with golden glazed rims. In these last four days, the Southern Pacific Hotel had been a pleasant diversion from the brown and dusty world around him.

After dinner the idle chatter of their conversation turned to the local climate, the Indians, and gold and silver mining in general. The sort of small talk two people who do not know each other very well employ to change that situation. During it, the three women made their way out of the dining room and traced a crooked path across the lobby toward the hotel bar. Mandell signed the check when it came and took Rose by the arm.

In the lobby Rose Haven turned to face him, and he was surprised to only now notice how tall she was. For a brief moment he imagined her beneath the bulk of her dress and jacket and hat. Long legs and arms, slender waist, her hair freed of its pins . . .

He extinguished those thoughts before they could begin to flame.

"Thank you for a lovely evening, Mr. Mandell."

"It is you I must thank. You are a flower in this bleak land, and I most enjoyed sharing the time with you."

She smiled demurely, then made a small, delightful laugh. "I'm certain the sun and heat of this place have affected you, Mr. Mandell. But the words sound nice just the same."

"Will I see you tomorrow?"

Her shoulder rolled slightly as she turned toward the hallway that led to her room. "Yuma is a small place, and the boat even smaller. The possibility is quite good, I should think."

"They serve a passable breakfast in the dining room."

A slight lifting of an eyebrow, and a smile was her reply. "Good night."

"Good night, Miss Haven."

She started down the hallway, and when her green bustle had disappeared around a corner, Harrison Mandell heaved in a huge breath as if he had been holding it all evening. All at once the long trip upriver did not look so bleak.

Like coming down off a high mountain, his ears suddenly opened, and he became aware of the noise around him and the laughing voices issuing from the hotel bar. It was still too early for bed. Shoving his hands into his pockets, he turned his steps toward the happy, intoxicated sounds.

9

"I heard the man was run off the Mississippi River and he was lucky the company didn't put out a warrant. Heard there was no solid proof right off. And once there was, he'd slipped into the territory, it was too much trouble to go after him."

"So they just let him go?"

The first man had the shoulders of a dock worker: Muscles plumped into shape by heavy work rippled beneath the red union shirt and dirty suspenders when he shrugged. He tasted his beer and said, "What else could they do? Like I said, there was never any good proof, only the word of a stevedore, and he weren't exactly reliable."

His friend was built along smaller lines. Grease under his fingernails and around the shoulders of his shirt suggested to Mandell that he worked around and inside engines. Steamboat boilers? The man propped his elbows on the bar to study the way the lamplight reflected through his whiskey, and Mandell couldn't tell if the frown was directed at some bug that had drowned in his drink or the thought that had formed in his head. "The captain is bad-tempered, but I never figured him for a thief. If this rumor gets out he'll have the law breathing down his backside."

The man in the red union shirt gave a snort and spilled some more warm beer down his throat. Mandell picked up his whiskey and carried it down the bar a little closer, stopping near the two men and casually looking out over the crowded barroom.

A woman's shrill laugh rose among the crowd and carried over the other noise. Across the room Darlinda stood up, considerably less steady on her feet than the last time Mandell had seen her. She flung her arm around the waist of a portly gentleman no less sober. Hidden among her grand display of undivided attention toward this man, Mandell caught the quick shrewd glance and the unspoken communication that passed between her and the older woman. Then she and her gentleman friend staggered out the door into the hotel lobby and away somewhere.

"— talking with Alf Danderfault, the fireman on the *Bad Water*. He says the man is a bear to work under, 'specially when he gets to drinkin'."

Mandell focused his attention back to the conversation at the bar.

The smaller man had produced a pocket

knife and made vague advances toward cleaning his dirty nails while he considered this. "Well, I can't say it ain't true, but just because a man has a reputation for driving his crew like they was black slaves don't mean he's somehow crossways with the law."

The first man lifted his beer, made a sour face, and pushed the mug away. "I've had enough of this swill."

Mandell grinned into the whiskey in his glass. Unlike beer, it didn't have to be cold to taste good.

"It's no secret he hates the river."

"That's no crime. If it were, half the folks in Yuma would be in jail." The mechanic slipped the knife back into his pocket and went back to studying his drink.

"The point is, if he hates it so much, why does he stay? A man with his experience could get himself a job most anywhere — unless . . ."

"Unless he was blackballed from working anyplace worth working at?" the second man suggested.

"Exactly. So, at the very least, there must be some truth to the story."

"Maybe." He stuck a dirty finger into the whiskey, fished around a bit, then pulled the finger out and squinted at a black gnat stuck to the tip. "If you told me he punched his mother in the nose I'd have no problem believing it. But embezzling forty thousand dollars from a steamboat company, well . . . I have no particular love for Alexis Patronoff, but before I ever accused the man of that, I'd need a lot more proof than the word of a second cousin, heard from a friend, picked up from someone comin' down the Mississippi River." He flicked the insect away and wiped his finger on his shirt sleeve.

The other man gave a short laugh. "I'd never accuse him either — at least not to his face."

Both men laughed and nodded their heads. Finally here was something they could agree upon.

"And besides," the second man continued, "if he did have the forty grand, why would he stay on the river? Answer me that?"

Mandell stepped up beside them at that point. "Evening, gents. I'm new here in Yuma."

The one with the strong shoulders glanced over. He looked Mandell up and down, grinned, and said, "Pretty obvious. Clothes like those don't last long in this part of the country."

Mandell gave him back an easy grin. "I couldn't help but overhear what you gents were talking about."

The man's expression hardened. "So, what of it? It's a free territory."

Mandell nodded at the beer abandoned on the bar. "Pretty poor beer they serve up.

Haven't found any yet worth drinking, and in the last four days I've tried just about every place around. But I did spy a bottle of Glenlivet tucked away behind the bar. I think the bartender intends to keep it for himself. If you gents are interested in some friendly conversation, I'm buying."

Their eyes brightened. In a glance they assented that they might be interested. Mandell flagged down the bartender, slapped a gold piece onto the bar, and got a dusty quart bottle in exchange. He didn't think these gents were up to the pleasures of Glenlivet, and as he carried it to a vacant table in the corner, he half regretted that McPeevy wasn't around. The Scotsman at least would have appreciated it.

Harrison Mandell had been living out of a fully packed suitcase since his first day in Yuma . . . and, apparently, so had all the other passengers bound upriver on the *Bad Water*. When the next morning Captain Patronoff pulled the whistle ring five times, he had but to toss a few items into his bag and buckle it closed and he was on his way down to the desk to check out. A staggering headache from the night before slowed him a bit, but just the same, by the time he arrived, a line had already formed, and he fell in behind McPeevy. He was mildly surprised to discover that at the head of the line were the three women. The older one was taking care of business, as, Mandell mused, she probably did in other matters as well, while the redhead and her companion stood nearby with bags sitting at their heels.

McPeevy had a pile of luggage at his feet, and a strange-looking bag of red and black tartan, the likes of which Mandell had never seen before.

"I see you found King Robert."

"Aye. The poor beastie was up an alley about to dig himself to Australia. I haven't yet thanked ye for stopping that ruffian with the gun."

"An old tomcat was poor sport. I just gave him a bit more challenging distraction."

McPeevy laughed. "Aye. So I heard later. A deputy United States marshal it was."

Mandell made a rueful smile. "How was I to know?"

"You might have asked." McPeevy's muttonchops spread apart with a grin to show that he was only joking. "And on a different matter, how did your dinner engagement with the lass from San Diego go last night?"

"It turns out she is from San Francisco. And dinner went fine."

"Hmmm?" McPeevy studied him a moment. "But ye do not look so fine."

"The bartender cheated."

"Oh?"

"He took a fine old scotch bottle and filled

it with rotgut from one of his bulk barrels. Charged me full price for it too."

"You drank the stuff?" McPeevy sounded truly amazed. "Can ye not tell true scotch from that stuff they distill in Taos, or wherever it is they concoct it?"

"Certainly. But I didn't want to let my guests know we'd been hoodwinked."

"Guests?"

"Never mind. It's a tale best told after a little time has taken off the rough edges."

Then it was McPeevy's turn at the window.

While Mandell waited for the Scotsman to close his account, Rose Haven came down the hallway carrying her carpetbag. She smiled when she saw him and stepped in line.

"Good morning, Miss Haven," he said. "It doesn't look like there will be time for breakfast after all."

"It doesn't matter, really. I'd rather be on our way." She appeared bright and fresh. Happy this morning, he thought, wearing a brown, velvet-trimmed traveling dress and narrow-brimmed tan hat with a wide ribbon of matching material. She carried a folded-up parasol — protection from the sun, presumably, as Mandell didn't fancy the danger from rain to be very great — and a leather handbag over her shoulder.

"Sleep well?" he asked as she set the bag

on the floor and extracted a coin purse from the handbag.

"Yes, and you?"

Mandell thought of the bottle of bad whiskey and gave her a wry smile. "Turned out to be a long night."

She looked at him questioningly, but then it was his turn at the window, which he promptly relinquished to her.

Her bill settled, he was next. Afterward he carried his bags outside onto the porch where she had paused to wait for him. From down on the river the five short whistle blasts from the *Bad Water* was repeated.

In the roadway ahead McPeevy had taken the lead down to the docks, with the three women hurrying as close behind him as fast as their skirts would allow, struggling with more baggage than they had arms to carry conveniently.

Mandell and Rose started after them. They hadn't gone but a few paces when a movement out in the desert, beyond the Southern Pacific tracks, drew his eye. A rising cloud of dust thrown up by a number of horses billowed toward the road. The horses came suddenly to a stop, and a band of Indians slowly emerged from the settling dust. They lingered there and debated some matter of contention, pointing and jabbering. A man with an ancient face and long white hair, slicked back with what looked like mud, apparently was trying to get some point across to the young man next to him. This younger fellow was nearly naked, his own black hair streaked and packed with red mud. Red mud smeared his cheeks as well and made criss-cross marks on his bare, hairless chest.

Mandell recognized the young Indian at once and glanced down at the redhead who at that moment had noticed them too. She dropped her baggage in the road, grabbed up her skirts and crinoline, and with a shriek to match the *Bad Water*'s piercing steam whistle broke into a run.

This brought the Indian's discussion to a prompt halt. With a yelp, the young buck heeled his horse and started down toward the river. The older Indian shook his head, and he and the others followed along at a more leisurely pace.

Mandell and Rose quickened their step. He paused long enough to hand Rose her bag back and collect the discarded bags and tuck them under his arms along with his own. Looking like an overworked porter, waddling a bit now beneath the burden of the extra luggage, the detective made his way down to the boat.

Darlinda dashed past everyone else on the road and rushed out onto the dangerous pier, a heartbeat ahead of the Indian, heedless of missing planks and gaping holes. The young Indian reined to a halt, blocking the way of the two other women and McPeevy, who had been passed by as if standing still.

A moment later the rest of the Quechans arrived, and Mandell too, dropping the luggage and shouldering into the shuffle — naked legs, arms, and flailing elbows everywhere — mud-streaked hair and bodies, smelling like a wrestling match attended to with much liquor. Mostly the Indians were grinning, and mostly the grins showed missing teeth. He discovered that among the men were two women; one old, one young, painted in mud, hair matted, virtually indistinguishable from the men except for the presence of naked breasts and grass skirts instead of leather breechclouts.

The Indians paid him no attention as he made his way through them and stepped onto the rickety dock.

Captain Patronoff came down the gangplank and snagged the redhead who, it seemed if left to her own devices, would have continued her flight clear off the far end of the pier.

"Here! What is it?" Patronoff rumbled, his fierce black beard thrust forward, his dark eyes narrowed in the brilliant sunlight.

"Keep . . . keep that crazy Indian away from me!" she cried, struggling to break free of Patronoff's grasp.

He hefted the girl under his arm like a sack of grain and came forward, his cigar a puffing steam engine, his black boots thumping the pier like pistons. "What the hell is going on here?" he demanded, taking in the entire group in a single glance. And a growing group it was. The madam and her girl, eleven Indians, McPeevy, three curious Mexicans with saddlebags over their shoulders and rifles in their hands, Mandell himself . . . and, Mandell noted with a bit of curiosity, the deputy U.S. marshal from the saloon the day before. Long legs carried the lawman to the edge of the pier where he drew up and gave Mandell a tight, expressionless stare. His face was blue and puffy, and a blood-encrusted bandage had been taped rather carelessly across his chin. He viewed Mandell through a single good eye, the other being swollen shut, until the captain's rumbling voice pulled that eye back to the drama unfolding on the pier.

"Well? Either out with it, or get the hell off my dock!"

The older Indian drew in a breath. He gave the younger man beside him a look of impatience that was clear in any language, then slid off the side of his horse and stopped in front of Patronoff.

The captain shifted his view. "So, it's you, Chief. What is it now? I ain't taken none of your ferry trade away from you now, have I?" Patronoff chuckled, as if taking away the Indian's trade would be great sport if he could.

The chief shook his head. Mud braids hissed like rattlesnakes along his back. "No, Captain. Business good. And you?"

Patronoff nodded his head. "I do all right, but you didn't come here to discuss business — least I hope not — not under this damned sun."

The chief grinned gap-toothed. "Yes. I have come to talk business, Captain."

"Oh, hell!" Patronoff glowered and slapped a mosquito on his wrist.

The Indian leveled a questioning glance back at the younger man. Even to an untrained eye it was clear the two men were related — father and son. The younger one grinned and nodded his head eagerly. Mandell detected a shrug of resignation in the old man's shoulders as he turned back to Patronoff.

"I want to buy woman for my son."

"You want to what?" Patronoff bellowed.

The redhead cringed back, shaking her head, on the verge of a swoon.

The Indian shrank from Patronoff when the captain leaned forward.

"I have money — white-man money."

"No doubt, you scoundrel. I know what you charge to ferry folks across the river." Patronoff considered the chief, then said, "How much money?"

"What?" the madam protested, pushing her way past Mandell, momentarily drowning out the odor of the Indians with her own pungent-sweet aroma, heavily subdued beneath the scent of tangy toilet water, but making itself known in the heat just the same. "You can't sell Darlinda!"

Patronoff laughed.

The chief said, "Twenty-five dollars, hard American money. Gold."

Patronoff grunted. "I don't know, Chief. She's kinda scrawny. Don't know as I'd feel right taking your money for the female."

The chief's son grinned and began to gyrate eagerly on the back of his horse.

"What the hell does your son want with a white gal anyway?" Patronoff nodded at the two bare-breasted, mud-painted females straddling the sweaty horses. "Why when he got such lovely women of his own people would he want this bony woman?"

The chief touched his own head, then pointed at Darlinda's head. "The hair, like sun going down."

Patronoff looked at Darlinda as if only now noticing the fiery red tresses. "You want her for her hair?"

The boy nodded with ingenuous anticipation.

The stomp of a heel on the pier cracked like a firecracker. "You can't buy her," the madam said. "At least not that way," she added with what Mandell thought was an equally ingenuous eye at the money pouch on the old man's waist.

"Molly!" Darlinda cried, coming momentarily out of her half swoon.

Molly took a firm stance. "Darlinda is not for sale. You Indians, you just turn around and go away. Shoo — shoo."

"You heard her," Patronoff said. "The gal ain't for sale."

The chief ignored Molly, keeping his dark eyes on Patronoff. "No make deal with woman. Make deal with man. You, Captain. Forty dollars."

"It's mighty tempting, Chief." At that moment he spied the lawman down among the crowd. His grin vanished like morning river mist. He stiffened and released the redhead. She scampered along the pier, up the gangplank onto the *Bad Water*, and disappeared among the hills of cargo there. "You'll have to go find yourself another redhead somewhere else." The discussion was at a close and Patronoff wheeled away.

"Captain," the chief called.

The bearded man strode onto the boat and was gone. The crowd broke up. Disappointed Indians turned away. Molly and the quiet girl gathered up their luggage and carried it aboard. The Mexicans and McPeevy boarded too. The lawman grabbed up a leather bag, stabbed Mandell with a stare from his single good eye while Rose stepped past him.

Harrison Mandell was suddenly alone on the edge of the pier in the heat and the bugs. He hefted his bags and boarded with the others.

10

With a shudder that ran through the boat like the first shakings of an immense beast awakening from a deep sleep, the great paddle wheel began to turn, tasting the water in broad, shallow bites, backing the *Bad Water* away from her moorings and out into the river. Men tossed off lines and spun them expertly into compact spirals on the deck. Black smoke billowed, obscuring the relentless sun for a blessed moment while steam hissed from escape pipes and pistons plunged, sending power surging along the connecting rods to the paddles behind.

He was *finally* on his way. Mandell leaned over the railing watching the pier slip from view behind the pivoting bow, feeling a fine spray off the paddle wheel that when caught in a breeze, cooled the brow as well as helped keep the bugs at bay.

"Damn almighty hot, ain't it?"

Molly stopped by the railing beside him. She looked miserable, laden with petticoats and a heavy dress, fanning herself with a piece of stiff paper. When she smiled she appeared ever so much like a painted doll, and

Mandell was grateful to be upwind of her.

"My name is Molly Sinclair."

"Harrison Mandell." He took her hand.

Molly dragged her two companions around as if a proud mother showing off a pair of shy children. She slung her arms over their shoulders. "These here are my girls, Betty Deland and Darlinda Madison."

He tipped his hat. "Pleased to meet you, ladies."

The redhead smiled widely, invitingly. The other, a brunette with pretty blue eyes, offered merely a hint of a smile and then immediately directed her attention to the churning trail of water behind the big wheel.

"I believe I've seen you around town, Mandell." She looked him up and down with little shyness. "Right handsome fellow you are."

He grinned. "I have noticed you and your girls as well."

Molly's laugh was like a donkey's bray. "I'll bet you have. That little show the other day in the middle of the street, I'll wager. Imagine that aborigine wanting to buy my Darlinda!"

Mandell glanced at the woman in question. It *was* hard to imagine, but wipe off half of the facepaint and do something sensible with her brilliant hair and she might be attractive.

"So, Mandell, you are heading for the mine too?" she asked.

Molly allowed her girls to wander away. She had showed him her wares, now it was time to make the sale. But he couldn't evoke much interest and found attention drifting, his view returning to linger along the high desert bluffs above the river. He repeated the story he'd been telling since he had arrived in Yuma. Molly seemed only vaguely interested, and when he had finished she told him the Bad Water Mine used to be ripe pickings for an enterprising madam and her girls, but then the men began to marry and bring their wives in, and the trade petered out. But Molly figured there was still enough unattached gentlemen left at the mine to turn a profit.

"You married, Mandell?"

He remembered Joan Pinkerton chiding him on that account. *You're thirty-five, Harry, it is about time you find yourself a nice girl,* she had said on his last visit. He grinned wryly to himself and wondered if Allan would readily agree to put him out to pasture just because he had found himself a *nice* wife. No, while he worked for Allan, it was better he stayed single. He had decided that a long time ago.

"I am not married, Miss Molly."

"Just call me Molly," she said, and poked him companionably in the shoulder with hard knuckles. "You will have to come by my place once I get it set up." She winked a most unladylike wink and went on in a lower voice, "Of course, if you can't wait, we can arrange for you to get to know my girls before then."

"I will keep that in mind, Molly," he said.

Suddenly Darlinda was at the madam's side and panic was in the girl's face.

"What's wrong?" Molly asked. "Get a grip."

Darlinda pointed to the river bluffs where a band of Indians had appeared. "It's him!" she cried, waving a finger in the general direction of the Arizona shore. At this distance it was impossible to determine which Quechan it was that Darlinda was attempting to indicate.

Molly tried to comfort the girl. "You're safe here. They can't get to you whilst you is on this boat. Ain't that right, Mandell?"

"I should think Captain Patronoff will do his best to keep the Indians off of his boat," he said, but that didn't seem to ease Darlinda's trepidation any. It did, however, give Mandell an excuse he needed to extradite himself from Molly's sales pitch. "I will inform the captain immediately." He tipped his hat and left.

The pulsing of the *Bad Water*'s engines was like a heartbeat pumping through the steamboat, turning the eighteen-foot paddle wheel twenty revolutions a minute, driving the boat upriver against a seven-knot current. Its rhythm remained dead steady. *Chukety pow,* chukety pow, chukety pow. And like a heartbeat, after a few minutes Harrison Mandell was no longer aware of it. He climbed the wide steps to the boiler deck, then a narrower set of stairs up to the hurricane deck where the wheelhouse was perched.

The wheelhouse was a cozy place, sealed up tight as a bank, filled with smoke from Patronoff's cigar. The captain was scowling through the spokes of the helm, puffing madly, while a second man, Tommy Morgan, had a pair of binoculars to his eyes, scanning the river ahead.

Tommy Morgan was a slender gent, appearing taller in his slenderness than actual fact. He had a bald head surrounded with a graying fringe of hair that hung down to his shoulders and gold-rimmed spectacles perched on a narrow nose. Tommy Morgan gave the appearance of a man forever making entries in a thick, black book; marking time and date, referring always to a silver watch he carried in a vest pocket. And when he wasn't marking entries, he was studying the way the water moved ahead of the boat through his field glasses. He was Patronoff's assistant — or perhaps he was the pilot — the man's job was not yet clear to Mandell, but it did seem that Tommy was the man Patronoff charged with the more important tasks.

Patronoff craned his neck when he came through the door, deepened his scowl at seeing him there, and immediately returned his attention to the river unfolding between the twin black smokestacks ahead.

"Indians are following along on the bluffs," Mandell mentioned casually.

Patronoff kept his attention ahead, as if he hadn't heard. Tommy Morgan put the glasses momentarily on them then let the binoculars drop to his chest. "They do that sometimes," he said, clearly distracted, referring back to his black book then the silver watch. "They get a kick out of it. It don't take much to entertain them."

It was clear his presence was not appreciated. Mandell strolled out onto the hurricane deck in front of the wheelhouse where he had a wide view of the river. Tinted red with silt of mountains as far north as the Wind River Range in Wyoming, the river for the moment flowed sedately in a wide channel between high bluffs. But Mandell knew that danger lurked mere inches beneath the surface. Hidden sandbars and snags could reach out anytime and catch the boat or, worse, rip open her hull. And even his novice eye was able to pick out the eddies and ripples that warned of shallow water.

He glanced back at the wheelhouse. Sunlight glinting off the windowpanes prevented him from seeing inside, but he knew Patronoff and Morgan would be watching for the warning signs too.

Chan Loo came up the stairs and smiled at him. "Mr. Manderr, you likee sometin' to drink?"

Mandell glanced at the pitcher of tepid tea on the tray that the Chinese handyman was taking to the wheelhouse. "Thanks, Chan, but what I need right now is a cold beer."

Chan's grin widened and his eyes narrowed further. Mandell wondered fleetingly if they didn't in fact close completely. "No gotee beer on board. Sorry, sorry. The other pass'gers down in main cabin. The bar is open."

"The bar is open?"

Chan bobbed his head. "I takee this to capt'n now." He hurried on his way, around the corner of the wheelhouse.

Mandell gave a final glance at the Indians on the bluff whose pace, it seemed, now precisely matched that of the boat. He fanned away a swarm of black gnats that had managed to find him and went down to the main cabin.

11

As Captain Patronoff was ever quick to point out, the *Bad Water* was not set up to carry passengers. It had none of the luxuries of the big packets that plied the waters of the Mississippi River. There were no guest cabins, no spacious gambling salons, no exquisite dining rooms with their white-clad waiters and quartet of stringed instruments playing unobtrusively somewhere in the background.

The *Bad Water* had none of that. It was a workhorse, built along the lines of an upper Missouri boat: shallow of draft, lean as a ringfighter, with powerful engines and deck accommodations stripped down to bare minimum. The *Bad Water* was a solid, sleeves-rolled-up breed of boat.

The few concessions made for human passengers seemed almost grudgingly given. There were three cabins on the main deck: the captain's, Chan and Loo Han Ling's, and a locked storage room where the crew kept their warbags. The crew did not sleep on board, but in shore camps along the bank; the Colorado was far too treacherous a river to negotiate in the dark. Those who preferred to sleep on the boat did so wherever there was room enough to stretch out. Because they were married, Chan and Loo Han Ling had the only accommodations that might reasonably be called private, and did not serve in some fashion as a common room. The captain's quarters were semiprivate, serving concurrently as a storeroom for the spirituous cargo and medical supplies and as a makeshift infirmary when the need arose.

Mandell learned most of this from Loo Han Ling, whom he encountered on the staircase on his way down. She was young, much younger than her husband, pretty in an Oriental fashion, and spoke almost perfect English.

"The mission school in Tientsin," she had told him when he inquired. "My mother died when I was very young, and Father could not care for all of his children and work the rice paddies at the same time, so we lived at the mission school where the Jesuit priests taught us English . . . and Latin as well."

After the mission school she resided a few years on a fishing boat and then spent six years as an actress with the Beijing Repertory Company before working her way to America as a cook on a tramp steamer.

Loo Han Ling left him at the boiler deck and went busily on her way. The door to the main cabin was open, and the windows too. Captain Patronoff would not have approved,

Mandell mused. The breeze that came through was slight, but it seemed to suit the mosquitoes just fine. At the moment the chairs around the long table held discarded jackets, hats, and bits and pieces of luggage — and a heat-weary Scotsman. More luggage and the steamer trunks were piled in the far corner along with a dozen canvas-and-wood cots — disassembled and rolled up like cordwood. A curtain was available to give the ladies a smidgen of privacy.

By one of the open windows the deputy U.S. marshal looked over; a drink in his hand, an indiscernible expression — nothing moved but his gray eyes as Mandell stepped up to the makeshift bar. The lawman's broad hat was hooked over a chair and the hateful sun through the window reflected off a receding hairline, picking out gray streaks in the tangled locks that hung below the man's shoulders.

Mandell gave him a grin and reached for a glass on the bar. The selection amounted mainly to four bottles of whiskey and six bottles of tequila. There was a jug of warm water and a small barrel of rocklike biscuits that reminded him of army hardtack. The lawman tossed back his drink and banged his glass down on the bar next to the one Mandell was about to fill for himself. The sound brought McPeevy out of a daze at the far end of the table. He fanned at a fly in front of his nose, gave the lawman a scowl, then glanced down at his valise. All in order. McPeevy leaned back in the chair, arms splayed, throat bared, and turned up as if sacrificing himself to the heat and the bugs.

In another chair, pulled away from the table and facing a window that looked out onto the high bluffs, the redhead sat locked in a hypnotic gaze. It took no great effort to know what Darlinda was staring at.

The rest of the passengers remained outside where at least the forward progress of the boat kept the hot air moving. He hadn't seen Rose since their departure, except for a glance of her strolling down the gallery toward the big paddle wheel astern.

The detective pulled the cork. "Whiskey?"

" 'quila," the lawman said.

He filled his own, uncorked a tequila bottle, and noticed a worm at the bottom of it as he filled the lawman's glass. A right happy worm, no doubt, he mused. The lawman didn't seem to mind wormy tequila. In a glance, Mandell discovered that all six tequila bottles contained resident annelids. No doubt a peculiar custom of distillers south of the border.

The lawman said, "You do pretty good with a right hook, mister."

"I was lucky."

"Maybe."

Mandell withdrew the nickel star from his

pocket and put it on the bar. "That belongs to you." He thought he heard a chuckle . . . but then maybe not. The lawman seemed to be laboring in his breathing. Not surprising. The humid river air was like a wet blanket, heavy on the chest, suffocating.

He pinned it back to his shirt, beneath the vest that hung open, and said, "The name's Dern Turnbough." He didn't offer a hand.

"Harrison Mandell."

Turnbough made a small sound in his throat, nodded his head, and without another word took his glass back to the window. His way of showing that although he had been bested once, he was not intimidated.

Turning back to the long room, the detective noticed that McPeevy had straightened up in his chair and was looking hard at Darlinda. Was that recognition he noted in the Scotsman's face, or only curiosity?

It struck Mandell odd that although this was a place full of people, it had the feel of a cemetery. Through the soles of his shoes came the pulsing heartbeat of the boat, and as if his senses had all at once intensified, he could almost see in some occult way the dip of each paddle as it came around to bite the river.

Mandell sipped his whiskey, but it didn't satisfy. What he wanted was a cold beer. He recalled with some fondness a small brewery that he had had the good fortune to discover.

What had been the name? He could not recall it now, but fate and Allan Pinkerton had come together in one of those rare moments to carry him to Black Hawk, Colorado, where he discovered the handiwork of a German brewer in the nearby town of Golden. Mandell put the thought out of mind. No sense torturing oneself. This was the Colorado River, after all, not Colorado, and as far as he knew, the beer wasn't available anywhere outside the state.

He glanced back at McPeevy. The Scotsman had stood, hesitantly, worrying the brim of his hat in his fingers, and then as if finally settling a struggle within him, stepped toward Darlinda.

From out of nowhere a hand had swung out and slapped the bottom of Mandell's glass, and suddenly the whiskey was in his face. Only . . . there had been no hand. Only a terrible, wrenching crunch. The floor beneath him lurched, and the *Bad Water* gave out a banshee's wail, heaving upward with a sickening screech of rock grinding beneath her keel.

Mandell grappled for the edge of the bar. The sudden shifting of the boat launched Dern Turnbough across the room. McPeevy lurched backward and flattened onto the table like a beached jellyfish. The valise carrying the King scudded along the tilting floor. Luggage, trunks, and cots *whoomp*ed against the wall, and Darlinda, in one startled moment, joined the merging of baggage — chair and all; her legs at once ceilingward, then starboardward, then coming full around in a direction more or less pointing forward.

Mandell's grip broke and he smacked a shoulder into the corner of the table. Momentum carried him on and flung him against the port-side wall of the cabin where everything else in the room seemed to be heading, gravity being the inexorable force that it was.

Wood twisted and moaned, joined now by the rising scream of a panicky woman and a yowling chorus from a most perturbed tomcat. Mandell groaned too and thought he heard a similar sound emerging from somewhere beneath him.

The boat settled back slowly, righted itself, and ceased its movement, but the floor did not feel quite level. He tossed a chair off of himself and levered himself up.

"Get your damned elbow out of my spine!" barked the man beneath him.

Mandell scurried off the pile of wreckage.

Clawing his way out of the pile, King Robert the Second gained his freedom too. Thoroughly confused, the cat took a moment to ponder the situation while securing himself firmly to Dern Turnbough's nose with mighty claws. Turnbough sputtered and began to sneeze. Mandell had a fleeting vision of justice well paid before shooing the cat off and giving the marshal a hand up out of the mess. He turned then to locate McPeevy floundering among the rubble, caught a flagging hand, and freed the Scotsman from the pile.

McPeevy sat heavily on the floor, bracing himself with both hands while Mandell rummaged around a bit more and came up with a very disheveled redhead who, like McPeevy, sought out a square of floor and secured herself to it.

"Everyone all right?" Mandell asked.

"Saints!" McPeevy exclaimed. "What happened?"

"Offhand, I'd say we ran aground. Hit a sandbar."

"I feel sick," Darlinda moaned.

Mandell was suddenly aware of the rattling, rasping sound behind him. He turned to investigate and discovered Turnbough buckled over on the floor, gasping for breath, his fingers gripping the front of his shirt, knuckles white as bleached skulls.

"Gilligan, help me get this man outside!" the detective said at once.

McPeevy clambered to his feet, and between the two of them they carried Turnbough out onto the tilting deck and sat him down in the shade on the gallery outside the starboard side of the main cabin.

"Saints, what be the matter with the man?"

"I've seen it before," Mandell said, working loose the top buttons of Turnbough's shirt.

Darlinda came out unsteadily and stood there watching, bracing herself against the boat's severe incline.

On the deck below, men with stout poles in hand scrambled toward the canted bow. Overhead, Patronoff's voice boomed. "Over to starboard. Put your backs to it, men."

Rose Haven climbed the tilted deck, coming forward along the gallery. Behind her, Mandell noticed the paddle wheel seemed to sit lower in the water. "We've run aground," she said, grabbing the railing for support. "What happened here?"

Down at the bow poles went into the water. Shoulders bulged and strained, glistening red and bronze under the sun.

"Tommy! Give me full reverse!" Patronoff called in a different direction.

Somewhere below a bell rang three times. The beat of the steam engine changed. Its drumming ceased for an instant, then resumed, and a shudder ran the length of the vessel. Aft, a frothy wash of whitewater boiled over the top of the paddle wheel.

Patronoff's fierce, bearded face appeared at the railing above. For a moment it seemed the captain intended to address them, but when he spoke it was clear his words were meant for someone on the deck below. "Alf! What does the boiler look like?"

Up came the reply. "We are all right down here, Captain."

Patronoff's face disappeared from the railing and footsteps pounded the staircase. The captain mounted the boiler deck without a break in stride and plunged down to the stairway to the main deck. At the bow he leaned forward to examine something in the water, then barked orders to the men there and rushed back toward the engine room.

Mandell looked at Turnbough. The man was breathing hard, but his eyes seemed to have cleared.

"How are you feeling?"

Turnbough swallowed and spoke as if a fist had closed about his throat. "I'm all right," he croaked, hiding his embarrassment beneath the cover of impatience.

"Rose," the detective said, "will you bring us some water?"

"Yes, of course."

Color was returning to Turnbough's cheeks, but his breathing was still harsh, and it was clear the best thing for him now was to remain right where he was, not moving.

Rose returned with a glass. Turnbough knocked away Mandell's hand and took it from her himself.

"I'm all right," he insisted again, wheezing.

"You are not," Mandell said, "but you will be in a few minutes. Just take it easy."

Turnbough's eyes came up sharply.

Mandell understood something now. He knew what could make a man hate cats so violently. And he also understood something else. A matter called pride. He glanced up at McPeevy and said, "Let's see if we can give the captain a hand. Turnbough is okay."

"Aye," McPeevy replied, not at all convinced.

Mandell stood. Rose caught him by the sleeve. "What can I do to help?"

"Stay with him. He'll be all right in a few minutes."

"But what happened — I mean . . . ?"

"Ask him yourself." Mandell offered Turnbough a hand up.

The lawman rejected it and stood shakily on his own, leaning back against the wall of the cabin. Life had returned to Turnbough's eyes and they sparked like gray flint at Mandell. He knew that this gaunt, proud man hated him for having seen him like this.

12

"Saints! I have never seen a grown man a-actin' like that afore."

Mandell and McPeevy went down the steps and headed forward where deckhands strained against long poles shoved into the river bottom.

"If King Robert was my cat, I'd keep him out of Turnbough's way. The King could very likely find himself the main course in a feast for the fish at the bottom of the Colorado River."

McPeevy stopped and shot a glance back up the stair at the main cabin. "He'd do that? Is the man sick or something?"

Mandell nodded. "I suppose in a way he is. He's asthmatic."

"Aye!" McPeevy suddenly understood. "He's allergic to cats!"

"I'd say that's putting it mildly," Mandell said as they made their way forward. At the railing, he peered over at the bow rammed up onto a spit of sand. "What can we do to help?"

One of the crewman glanced up and blinked sweat from his eyes. He didn't seem to notice the mosquitoes lighting on his bare back. "You can give me a hand at this," he said.

Both Mandell and McPeevy lent a shoulder, but they might as well have been pushing at a Pike's Peak. After a few minutes the engines stopped huffing and the big paddle wheel fell silent. Everyone immediately ceased pushing at the sandbar and slumped to the floor to recoup his strength and sling sweat from face and arms.

Captain Patronoff came forward from the engine room, climbed the wide steps on his way up to the wheelhouse. Mandell followed.

The Mexicans gathered by the closed door, looking worried. They stepped back out of Patronoff's way when he came through. "You can break free — no, *Señor* Captain?" asked the man who seemed to be the leader, Edwardo. His friends, Ramon and Felix, glanced about with concern in their faces.

Patronoff drove past them and shouted into a brass speaking tube near the helm. "Pressure stable, Alf?"

A voice came up the tube. "We are still all right, Captain. Plenty of water over the core."

That seemed to relieve Patronoff of some anxiety. He glanced at Tommy Morgan. "Think if we lighten the forward hold we can back her off?"

Morgan studied the river through a slip of green celluloid. First out at arm's length, then in nearer, then out again. "Must have been a slide up ahead somewhere," he mumbled to himself, glancing at the black book open in front of him as if to be sure. "This wasn't here a week ago." He considered the problem awhile longer. Patronoff was patient. He wasn't going anywhere and he knew it. Morgan came to his decision then. "It's too wide a shoal to grasshopper over. Afraid we are going to have to shift weight and try to back her off."

"I'll get the men to it." Puffing on the stub of a cigar, Patronoff wheeled about and discovered Mandell standing there. He stepped past him and was gone.

"You're the pilot, I take it?" Mandell said.

Tommy Morgan glanced over. "I'm the pilot."

"Can I help?"

"You can stay out of the way," Morgan said, not looking up. He shouted an order into the tube and put the binoculars to his eyes again, scanning the water. Frowning, he turned them up the side of the bluffs.

McPeevy peered into the wheelhouse. "Anythin' we can do?"

Mandell grinned. "We can stay out of their way."

"Right. If ye need me I'll be in the saloon." McPeevy scurried away before anyone could change his plans. The Mexicans said something in Spanish and they too went off somewhere.

"Damn savages," Morgan hissed, viewing the ridge through the field glasses.

Mandell squinted into the glare beneath the flat of a hand. He could see them up there, but the distance was too great to determine exactly what they were up to; dancing, perhaps?

"What's going on?"

Morgan gave him a peeved look, and his face showed color. He handed Mandell the binoculars and said, "They do it all the time. Great sport, they think. Follow the boats, they do." Morgan was unable to hide a bitterness that had apparently been festering a long time. He shoved the spectacles up the bridge of his nose and peered at a book of charts opened near the helm.

Mandell turned the glasses on the Indians, and it became clear what they were doing, and why the boat's pilot in particular would be embarrassed over it.

"They know where every damn shoal lies," Morgan went on, not looking up, "and they wait up there like buzzards until a boat runs aground on one. Damn fun, they think!"

Mandell couldn't help a low chuckle. The old chief and his impassioned son Olley and all the rest of the Quechans were up on the bluffs pointing, holding their sides, and reveling in one of the true pleasures of life — a roaring good belly laugh.

The detective returned the binoculars and went down to the main cabin where McPeevy had gotten himself roped into helping put the mess back in order, along with Molly and her girls. Rose seemed to have taken charge of the matter. Turnbough was shoving a heavy steamer trunk back in place, and whether or not he was recovered enough for the task made little difference. He plainly needed to prove himself, as if the attack of asthma were somehow his own personal fault.

Turnbough was not a man who would readily accept help, so Mandell didn't offer any as he too tackled one of the big trunks. Turnbough scowled. Mandell pretended not to notice and went right on restacking the baggage, hearing the ragged breathing of the man working next to him.

Afterward Mandell went down to the forward bow hatch where deckhands were handing up crates and carrying them aft like a line of busy ants. The captain monitored their progress from the bow and maintained a practiced eye at the sandbar and the steepening angle of the bow. Suddenly he said, "Enough there, boys," and waved a hand signal at the wheelhouse. In a moment a bell rang back at the engine room. Steam hissed, engines woke from their slumber, and the big paddle began to turn in reverse. The deckhands levered poles into the water and

Mandell lent a hand. Even Chan Loo joined in, dwarfed by the other men.

The boat shuddered, slipped back a notch. Captain Patronoff grabbed up a pole. The *Bad Water* slipped back another notch, and then the powerful paddle was pulling her free, dragging her back into deep water.

The deckhands were too hot and tired to raise a cheer. Wearily they dragged the poles up on deck and put them away.

Patronoff strode past Mandell, came to a stop, and turned back. The ubiquitous cigar was still stuck between his lips, but the fire had gone out of it. He puffed once to try to restart it, couldn't, and tossed it out into the river. He said, "The help was appreciated, Mandell. Thanks." He resumed his march up the stairs.

The hands went about the business of redistributing the *Bad Water*'s load with the efficiency of a well-seasoned troupe of circus roustabouts raising the big top, and Mandell had to wonder if running aground was a regular event. He stuck out an arm as Chan Loo came around a corner.

"Mr. Manderr," Loo said, coming up short, "veddy, veddy busy. Can no talkee now."

"I can see that, Chan. Does running onto sandbars happen often?"

Chan nodded his head. "Yes, yes. Tommee, he hittee more than he missee." Chan grinned and hurried off to help, but he left something behind. Mandell sniffed the hot air, and then again. Yes, he was sure of it now. Chan had been drinking . . . drinking beer.

13

"The man don't talk much, does he?" McPeevy said, leaning at the railing, watching the river splitting away from the bow in rolling V-shaped waves that broke on both shores far behind the steamboat. "I wonder what he is doing on board?"

"I haven't figured that out yet," Mandell said thoughtfully. "One thing you can count on. He has business up at the mine or Patronoff wouldn't let him come along. . . ." He made a wry face. "Or does he?" the detective added with a note of curiosity. Then he laughed. "I suppose we could just ask Patronoff."

McPeevy lifted the big cat from the valise at his feet and scratched it behind the ears. King Robert the Second's purring nearly masked the constant drumming of the steam engines.

"The marshal does not seem to like you, any more than he likes cats," McPeevy noted. He looked sharply past Mandell and lowered his voice. "Speaking of Patronoff, here comes the captain now."

Patronoff drew up by them, puffing out a

cloud of smoke from around the shaft of a fresh cigar. In the afternoon heat he looked fierce and swarthy behind the jungle of black hair. It struck Mandell just then that Alexis Patronoff would not be out of place at the helm of a tall sailing schooner flying the Jolly Roger.

"You gentlemen enjoyin' the trip?" the captain asked neutrally, as if it really made little difference to him. He spied the cat in McPeevy's arms and suddenly there was the ghost of a smile to his tight mouth. "And what have we here?"

McPeevy cleared his throat. "His name is King Robert the Second."

Patronoff dropped a big hand on the cat's head with a gentleness that might have been reserved for painted eggshells, rather than bone and scrappy fur. "Named after the Scottish king?"

"Aye! That he is, Captain."

The detective noted Patronoff suddenly rising in stature in McPeevy's eye.

"Fine-lookin' animal."

McPeevy beamed.

Mandell said, "Barring shoals and snags, when do you expect to make the mine?"

"Three days." Patronoff gave the cat a final scratch and looked at the river with distaste, taking the cigar between carefully manicured fingers. "But nothing is ever certain on the Colorado. A damn hell of a river. Not fit for man nor beast. It will never amount to more than dust and dry bones, and once the silver is played out the white man will give it back to the Indians . . . and the Mexicans." He glanced up at where the wheelhouse would be, although not visible from their location there on the boiler deck. Edwardo had chosen its tight confines to camp out in, and his constant inquiries were about driving Tommy Morgan mad.

"There is more in the ground than silver," Mandell said, recalling something he'd read in his dog-eared copy of *Fulbright's*. "Arizona is rich with copper."

Patronoff grunted. "Hardly any practical use for copper. Mark my words, once the silver is gone, the white man will leave too."

"Why do you stay?"

Patronoff gave Mandell a long, hard stare. "I got my reasons." His tone did not invite further inquiries. "Mark my word. You won't find me here in five years. That I promise you."

Mercifully, the sun dropped low on the horizon and evening came finally to the river, as if it had to fight and win a fierce battle just for the privilege. The day had sweltered long and valiantly, but at last it succumbed, defeated at the keen edge of the approaching night.

The *Bad Water*'s whistle echoed through

the sandstone escarpments that rose like walls to enclose them, and ahead, from around a bend of red and yellow cliffs, another whistle answered its call.

Rose had been telling Harrison Mandell about riverboats she had traveled on the Sacramento River, and of the Mexican family who cared for her father's horses, when the signal of the approaching boat clipped her words short. Every head in the stifling cabin turned to the port-side windows.

Mandell stepped outside where the encroaching evening did little to cool the air or lower the oppressive humidity. In the gloom ahead the gleam of a running light appeared around a rock outcropping, and then the shape of a steamboat emerged from the deep shadows. Whistles exchanged, the boat chugged nearer, and soon it became apparent this was a military vessel carrying troops down to Fort Yuma.

At the cabin door behind the detective Ramon had suddenly come alert, and had clutched up his rifle from which he never strayed very far. When Mandell turned, Ramon's sweaty face grinned back at him. It took no large imagination to know that one deck above, the leader, Edwardo, would be taking similar precautions in the wheelhouse.

The boats advanced on each other and edged near to opposite shores — but not too near. Mandell noted the shoals and snags there.

"They look all done in," Rose said as the boats passed with a scant twenty yards between them. The soldiers on deck in their blue wool uniforms waved in the weary fashion of men who had battled a malevolent sun all day and had been beaten insensible by it.

The passengers on the *Bad Water* returned the greetings with matched enthusiasm. The troop boat slid past and its bow wave rocked them gently but firmly. The water calmed and the two boats pulled back out into the middle of the river.

Behind him, Mandell sensed Ramon relaxing in the doorway. The Mexican let the rifle settle casually to the floor at his side where he gripped it by the barrel.

"I wonder how those poor men stand it dressed in such heavy uniforms," Rose commented as they returned to the cabin. But as they stepped past Ramon, Mandell was pondering a different question entirely.

Why had the Mexicans insisted on riding the *Bad Water*? He couldn't quite picture Edwardo, Felix, and Ramon as cooks for the mine, and grinned to himself at the thought.

There seemed to be more puzzles on this one trip than the detective could ever remember encountering all in one place, and being naturally a curious sort, his Pinkerton-trained brain, in its own peculiar and methodical manner, decided the time had come to start picking the problems apart.

14

Nighttime on the Colorado River: humid, bug-infested misery — the rigors of the day merely giving way to another kind of torment. A smoky fire produced a margin of relief, but short of wrapping oneself in mosquito netting, there was no escaping the "wee beasties," as McPeevy called them.

The *Bad Water* had heaved to and tied up when evening enveloped the river. Where she sat, a dozen feet off shore, the soft glow of scattered lanterns presented a disjointed picture. Before full darkness had covered the bleak land, Mandell had helped the deckhands in the wood gathering to replenish the boat's supply. The boiler had a voracious appetite. Alf Danderfault told him that the one major obstacle to steam travel on the Colorado was the consummate lack of something suitable to burn — and each year the problem worsened. Eventually, steamboats would incinerate their way out of business, leaving the barren landscape even more inhospitable than when the steamboat had first arrived on the river.

Across the way Captain Patronoff drew on his cigar, and the ember lent a sinister red glow to a face already deep in blackness. He had been speaking to two men, and now he walked toward the gangplank. Mandell set the tin coffee cup aside.

"That troop carrier was the only boat I've seen so far this trip," Mandell said. "Is there no regular passenger service this far north?"

Patronoff looked around, surprised to find the detective standing there behind him. "The army makes regular runs between Yuma and one or two camps up north," he said. "Yuma has been a major resupply point since the war. You'll most likely see more before we arrive at the Bad Water Mine. Passenger packets too possibly, although there ain't a whole lot of commerce in hauling people up and down the river. Mostly supplies, for the temporary army camps, and the mines, and the few towns what got the gumption to put down roots in this land."

Mandell brought the topic around to the real reason he had tailed the captain up the gangplank. "Any idea yet what our Mexican friends really want?"

Patronoff looked out across the blackness where here and there lamplight rippled on the water. "They want to go up to the Bad Water Mine."

"I don't think so, and neither do you. Edwardo keeps himself glued to the wheelhouse like a new stamp, and Ramon and Felix are never more than two steps from their rifles, no matter how casual they might act about it. I've watched them. They're strung up tighter than a rusty bolt."

Patronoff huffed. "Hell, Mandell, I don't know what they want — what they *really* want. And frankly, I do not much care so long as they don't make trouble aboard my boat. I got worries enough of my own." He stepped toward the staircase.

"You mean Turnbough?"

Patronoff wheeled, and in the darkness a flash of stray light from a nearby lamp glinted off the man's fierce dark eyes. "My business is none of yours. I'll thank you to stay clear of it. You put your nose where it don't belong, it's liable to come away bloodied."

Mandell had been fishing when he had asked about Turnbough. Now he held back the small grin of satisfaction. Patronoff had given him the answer to at least one of his questions. As the husky man turned back to the staircase, Mandell said, "Oh, by the way, Captain, I don't suppose there is any chance a person could get a beer on board the *Bad Water*?"

Patronoff, foot to the stair step, hand on the railing, paused only long enough to bark his reply. "We have none aboard this trip. Good evening, sir."

The main cabin seemed a gloomy place despite the lamps overhead and on the walls.

Molly and her two girls had a game of gin rummy going on one end of the long central table. Shredded cattails — the plant, not the King's — smoldered in a copper pot on the table, filling the room with smoke, ostensibly to drive away the mosquitoes . . . or at least that is what Chan Loo claimed they were supposed to do. No one yet, it seemed, had gotten around to telling the mosquitoes.

The three Mexicans hunched near the door like a gathering of vultures, passing a tequila bottle among them. Mandell looked around for McPeevy, but the Scotsman was not among the passengers there. Turnbough and Rose Haven sat at the near end of the table, the marshal with a glass of tequila, Rose with a cup of tea that Loo Han Ling had offered around earlier. Mandell poured himself a whiskey and carried it over.

"The marshal was just telling me all about his work here in Arizona. Law enforcement sounds like it would be very interesting."

"Like mining?"

She smiled and said, "No. But in its own way, quite alluring and glamorous."

Turnbough laughed — carefully — his face was still too sore for a real laugh. "I thought so too once upon a time. But look as I might, I never did find much *glamour* in it. Not nearly enough to make up for the cold meals, long hours, bedding down on hard or wet — or both — ground, and cantankerous horses."

"There is that, I suppose," she said sweetly.

Mandell said, "What brings you to the Bad Water Mine, Marshal? Business?"

Turnbough's expression clouded. He hid it momentarily in his tequila. "Personal reasons." It was clear that was how he wanted it kept.

"I reckon business of one sort or another brings most of us. Engineering, teaching —" Mandell glanced at Molly. "— all kinds of businesses. Have you been in Arizona long, Marshal?"

"Not too long. I come west for the weather."

"Because of your asthma?"

Turnbough speared Mandell with a narrow glance that warned not to pry too closely.

"It's no shame," the detective went on glibly. "I have an uncle with asthma. He used to live in St. Louis . . . until the heat and humidity like as not killed him. The doctor told him to either move to a different climate or invest in a plot. Ended up in Santa Fe. Works in a haberdashery on San Francisco Street and the asthma hardly ever bothers him now."

Turnbough set his glass down and thought it over some. "Missouri is a killer if you got the disease, that's for sure. The whole damned Mississippi Valley for that matter," he said with conviction. For an instant he allowed a grin to break through his severe face, then he buried it again among his thoughts.

"How long did you live on the river?"

"Most my life."

"Then you are probably familiar with these paddle boats — more so than I, or Miss Haven."

Rose was studying him curiously. Caught off guard by his remark, she regrouped and said, "I'm sure Marshal Turnbough is. My only experience is once or twice on the Sacramento River."

Turnbough glanced around the main cabin as if viewing it with a professional's eye. "I'd say I know these boats —" He was about to elaborate, then caught himself and said instead, "The Sacramento River is a busy place. Not like the Mississippi, but certainly a friendlier river for steamboaters than the Colorado."

"Were you a lawman back east?"

"No," he said, and again it was plain he didn't care to discuss too closely the details of his life. All at once Turnbough's head snapped up and he said, "What the hell is that noise?"

They all heard it, a haunting wail that drifted up from back near the paddle wheel, intruding itself upon the quiet river. But it wasn't wailing at all . . . it was music. Mandell recognized it then for what it was, but before he got the word out, Rose exclaimed:

"Bagpipes!"

"Could have fooled me. I'd have sworn it was the damned crying from their graves," Turnbough said.

At the other end of the table Molly and the girls put aside their cards. There was curiosity on two of their faces — Darlinda's, however, revealed something quite different. Her eyelids had suddenly compressed, with lines of concentration etching themselves in her forehead. Her view shifted out into space, as if the sound of the pipes had evoked a memory. A dangerous memory. She looked swiftly about. Her view glanced off of Mandell and settled on Dern Turnbough.

Mandell was aware that he had been staring in that same way Rose found most curious. He shifted his view to Turnbough and said, "Give you two guesses."

"McPeevy?"

Outside on the dark gallery they all piled to a stop. Upon the stern of the boiler deck, in front of the uppermost paddles of the stilled wheel, a shadowy apparition marched back and forth, looking oddly contorted in the chalky moonlight: black horns growing up his back, a dark hump bulging beneath his arm.

The sound of bagpipes swelled in the air, hauntingly, and continued on a sad strain until McPeevy noticed that he had attracted an audience. He lurched around and immediately ceased his playing, allowing mournful notes to die a slow death as the hump deflated.

"Saints! Ye startled me!" he proclaimed.

"We startled him?" Molly shot back playfully, looking at the others. "That horrible racket about made me drop my corset!"

The girls giggled.

"I think the music sounded just fine." This was Captain Patronoff, and his voice came from overhead. In the darkness on the hurricane deck above them, only the glowing tip of his cigar was visible. It described an arc that settled someplace in the vicinity of his mouth. "Please continue, McPeevy."

"Nae, I do believe the moment has left me," the Scotsman said, eyeing the crowd growing there on the boiler deck. "I think I will be a putting me pipes away now, if you please."

"I like it," Edwardo said, stepping out in front. "I have never before heard this sound. *Por favor*, play a little more."

"Ye did?"

"*Sí.*"

McPeevy cleared his throat. "Well, if ye insist." He put a length of pipe to his mouth and began to puff up the bag. A lively tune followed.

Molly tapped a toe on the deck. "Now, that's better," the madam said. "A happy sound for this weary group."

The quiet one, Betty, turned suddenly, took Mandell's hands, and stepped lively to the reel McPeevy was playing. It took Mandell off guard, cost him an awkward moment while his feet caught up. Then he was swinging the laughing woman out at arm's length, and in close, remembering steps long forgotten, relegated to a time when he was younger and life was less complicated.

In a moment all the women had been snatched up by the crew and whirled out onto the deck. More crew came up the gangplank to see what the excitement was about, swept up at once in the spontaneous gaiety. McPeevy finished the reel and started immediately in on another. The Loos were doing their own peculiar version of the dance, and even reserved Rose Haven found herself laughing and in the grasp of the big, sandy-haired Norwegian fireman named Alf. A mouth organ joined in making a most distinctive musical combination. No one seemed to care.

Felix tapped Mandell's shoulder and the detective relinquished Betty to the Mexican, who had no idea what a reel was but was enjoying himself immensely just the same.

Mandell stepped back where the crew and other passengers had gathered. Someone shoved a bottle of tequila in his hand. He looked over and saw Edwardo, grinning back at him.

"Thanks." He took a pull at the bottle, making certain beforehand that the worm at the bottom had disappeared. Probably down an unsuspecting throat.

"*Sí*. We have *muy grande* celebration tonight. Forget about the damned bugs, no?"

"Forget about them, yes." The detective took another drink, and was aware that the lawman had departed. He glanced along the shadowed gallery but saw only deeper darkness.

Out on the deck — now transformed into a dance floor — Ramon's sudden happy yelp brought the detective's thoughts back to the whirling couples. The Mexican had thrown his hat onto the floor and in an instant was leaping about it, dancing by himself, doing steps to music that must have been playing in his head, for the rhythm of his feet had absolutely nothing in common with the music coming from the pipes and mouth organ. But what the hell! Mandell grinned. The man was enjoying himself.

The crew members were taking advantage of the music and the supply of females aboard — rare commodities in this part of the territory. Chan and Loo Han Ling vacated the floor, both wearing big happy faces and breathing hard. From out of the darkness Captain Patronoff appeared at Chan's side. He bent and said something close to the Chinese man's ear, then retreated back to the shadows and down the starboard side gallery.

Chan whispered to his wife and left, making his way through the crowd. Mandell backed casually to allow him to pass and then, at a discreet distance, followed.

15

Mandell moved up to the railing above the staircase and waited. Below on the main deck, Chan's small figure disappeared in the shadows among the tarp-covered mounds of supplies and machinery destined for the *Mina del Agua Mala* mine. Mandell went quietly down the steps, melted into the darkness, and eased forward, keeping Chan in sight.

Chan went to the bow and glanced back over his shoulder at the upper deck where the impromptu dance was filling the quiet Colorado River with happy sounds. Mandell pressed against a hard, tarp-covered object, and only his eyes moved. The canyons through these stacks of cargo reminded him of the Chicago back alleyways that he had known while working for Allan Pinkerton. Aside from the location, there wasn't much difference between them and these canvas-covered piles.

The little man bent and heaved open the forward cargo hatch, and disappeared down it.

Mandell waited a few moments, and when Chan didn't immediately reappear, he went cautiously to the open hatch and peered down into the black rectangle. Scraping sounds from below reached his ears, grew fainter until they ceased and only the festive music back by the paddle wheel filled the night. He lowered himself through the hatch, contacting the floor five feet below, and stooped to clear the rafters that supported the main deck.

His eyes gradually adjusted to the dark, and the crates stacked about here and there emerged indistinctly from the gloom. A match flared far to the rear of the boat. Chan had lighted a lantern back there. Its light moved among the dusky shapes of cargo and whatever else a steamboat carried in its hold, and the detective had no idea what all should be down here.

He eased toward the light on hands and knees, more feeling his way along than seeing. The faint glow ahead did little to illuminate the way, merely a point to aim toward.

The music was muted here, below the cabins, and Mandell heard a metallic clatter, like a latch being thrown, and then the squeak of hinges groaned through the dark cargo hold. Something like a cupboard door slammed shut then, and a latch was shoved back in place. Mandell slithered behind a box as Chan came forward again, the light from the lamp in his hand leaping eerily from crate to crate, and along the bare ribs of the boat.

Suddenly the light went out.

Absolute blackness flooded back. There was the sound of the lantern being put away and then the faint scraping of Chan feeling his way forward.

Mandell pressed back against the beams of the boat as Chan came closer singing a quiet song beneath his breath; the words were unintelligible, but the melody seemed quite lively.

The sound of scraping was quite near now, and although in the blackness Mandell could see nothing, he sensed that Chan was very close — the singing clearer, perhaps an arm's reach away. And there was another sound — a clinking sound.

Mandell tried to identify it and could not immediately do so. The sound moved past him. The detective held his breath, listening to the clinking of . . . of . . . of bottles knocking one against the other?

The Chinese man passed the hidden detective unaware and made his way forward. In another minute the faint light through the bow hatch showed his silhouette suddenly clear in the moonlight, as if, to Mandell's dark-sensitive eyes, he had suddenly been caught in a photographer's flash.

Chan climbed up out of the hold and closed the hatch behind him, cutting off even that little bit of illumination.

Mandell sat back in the darkness frowning. He weighed his chances of making his way aft to investigate further, decided it would be useless tonight. He'd not be able to find the lantern, and even if he did, he had brought along no matches to light it.

When Mandell emerged on the deck, the sounds of dancing and laughter were still going strong. He brushed at his clothes and stretched out the cramps that had developed below. Up on the hurricane deck, two decks above, he recognized Chan's shuffling walk. Mandell made his way leisurely up the wide stairs and ascended the steps to the hurricane deck. He caught a glimpse of Chan in the light that came from the wheelhouse windows and drew up, his eyes just high enough to clear the top of the deck. Patronoff was there, and so was the marshal.

Chan gave each man a bottle and immediately left the wheelhouse. Mandell dove down the stairs and slipped behind one of the fat smokestacks as Chan turned a corner, heading back toward the party on the aft deck. When the Chinese man had gone, he made his way back to the wheelhouse, keeping to the shadows, and sidled up against the wall.

The two men's shadows stretched out on the deck in front of the wheelhouse. He watched them tipping the bottles up, heard their small sounds of satisfaction.

Then Patronoff spoke. "I think the man knows something!"

"How could he know anything?" Turnbough said. "No one knows — except you, and Tabor, and Tabor is dead."

Mandell detected a waver in Patronoff's voice. "I don't know. Maybe he don't. I keep hoping I have put enough distance between myself and that incident that I don't have to worry anymore." He paused, and then: "You're the only one left and once I'm free of you —" He left the sentence unfinished.

Turnbough laughed softly. "You got a conscience what's bothering you, that's all. Once you're free of me you can go on sweating out an existence on this river and stop worrying."

"Can I? Or do I go on watching over my shoulder all the time so's I don't get it like Tabor done?"

"Tabor and you, you two double-crossed me. Tabor didn't have what I wanted when I finally found him, and I could see no good reason to let him get away with what he'd done to me."

Patronoff grunted. "No, Tabor didn't have what you was looking for, but what he did have was my address."

"Suppose I ought to have thanked him."

"Instead you killed him. And what reason is there for you to let *me* get away with it?"

There was a note of humor in Turnbough's

voice. "I like you, Captain. I never did much care for Tabor and his 'better than thou' attitude. The son of a bitch's hands were as dirty as ours. But you were different. You never tried to make out you were any better than any one of us. Besides, I may have use of you in the future."

Patronoff laughed. "We may not have a future if Mandell knows something. He hinted as much earlier."

"There's no way. You're feeling guilt, and you're letting that regret make something out of nothing. Besides, the man is a mining engineer. What could he possibly know? What could he care? Me, on the other hand, I don't suffer from your problem. I never feel guilt."

Turnbough stepped out the wheelhouse door and looked around. Mandell held his breath as the lawman moved up beside him without seeing him crouched there in the shadows. Turnbough heaved back and threw the bottle out into the water. From the blackness came a small splash, and the lawman went back inside.

"Don't worry 'bout Mandell. If he does cause problems, I can take care of him."

Patronoff said, "You didn't do a very good job of it yesterday." A small note of satisfaction accompanied his words.

"Next time he won't know it's comin'. Not till a minute after he opens his eyes in hell."

Turnbough went to the door and turned back. "Patronoff. If you're even thinking of another double cross, forget it — unless you want to end up like Tabor. Have it ready for me once we make dock, and you won't be out nothing but money." He gave a short laugh. "You know, it's only the promise of that what's kept you alive this long." He stepped out the door and down the stairs.

Mandell caught a glimpse of him below in the lamplight as he took the stairs down to the main deck. A few moments later Patronoff stepped out too. He inhaled deeply, as if to clear his lungs. A match flared and the tip of his cigar took on a cherry glow again.

"Damn," he said softly, and flung his bottle overboard too.

Mandell watched the burly captain lumber down the stairs. Alone now, the detective made his way to the aft railing above the dancing and looked down on the next deck. The dance and pipe music was still going strong, but neither Patronoff nor Turnbough had joined in.

When Mandell returned to the party, Rose Haven's concerned expression at once brightened.

"Care to dance?" he asked.

"I'd be honored," she said.

"Where did you get off to?" she asked, smiling happily as he escorted her onto the floor.

"Oh, just took a stroll." He put the problem of Turnbough and Patronoff away for the moment, to enjoy Rose's suddenly smiling face, and the music.

He didn't know it then, but this night would be the last night that any of them would so freely put aside their caution.

16

When Gilligan McPeevy finally blew himself out on the bagpipes, the impromptu gathering dispersed like a drop of oil in soapy water. The crew headed ashore and to much-needed sleep. Molly and her girls took their leave in the main cabin on the other side of a curtain Chan Loo had drawn across the room for their privacy.

Mandell was drowsy, and he knew Rose was too, but it would have been a shame to retire now — the only part of the day when the sun and humidity wasn't assaulting them, or he wasn't slapping away the local wildlife. The stroll along the dark and quiet gallery was a pleasant change from the hectic day just past, especially since Rose did not appear overly eager to depart his side.

"My father told me I would hate this place," she said, stopping at the railing to look out across the black water. She glanced at him, a smile in her eyes. "And don't you tell me he sounds like a sensible man."

Mandell leaned on the railing listening to the river passing the moored boat. Most of the lamps had been extinguished, and only here and there a stray shaft of light reached out to touch the moving water. "Do you?"

She didn't answer him right away. When she did there was uncertainty in her voice. "I've always believed that a person can get along in most any situation so long as they wanted to. Father said I'd be home in three months, and that my room would be waiting for me."

"And he would arrange for a sensible teaching position at a proper San Francisco school?"

She laughed, but with no malice toward the man who had raised her. "More like to arrange a sensible position with a suitable young man. One of the juniors in his offices would suffice, thank you."

"Someone in particular?"

"I don't think so. Father made certain that I was properly introduced to every available one. I believe all that is required of me is to choose."

"You make it sound a little like shopping for a new dress."

She laughed again. "That is just about what it amounts to — at least to Father's way of thinking."

Mandell watched an undulating point of light out on the water awhile. "And you decided the *Mina del Agua Mala* was far enough away from your father's matchmaking to give you some breathing room."

She looked at him sharply. Then a small smile emerged. "You are far too clever for your own good, Mr. Mandell. But you are most incorrect. That is not the reason at all why I left home."

"I apologize," he said, thinking that her protest was a little too adamant. "Why did you come out to the Arizona Territory?"

"For the challenge, I suppose," she said thoughtfully. "Because San Francisco was safe and homey — but a little like a waist that had been left in the starch too long. Because, perhaps, when I do go back, as I surely will one of these days, one of those junior associates will ask for my hand, and I will accept. And then what? A nice house, children . . . ? My mother's life is about as exciting as an old dish rag. At least when I get to that point, there will be this to think back on. A bit of adventure. A smidgen of excitement. No other reason."

"Well, Miss Haven, you seemed to have picked the right boat to find excitement."

"Whatever do you mean?"

He grinned, delighting in her suddenly wide brown eyes. "Consider this. You've boarded a steamboat that, from what I've gathered, goes out of its way to run into shoals. On board is a captain who hates the river and longs for a past that he had lived on the Mississippi River, but to which he apparently cannot go back. An excitable woman of a shady occupation being hounded by a drunk Indian who is infatuated with the color of her hair. Three Mexicans armed as if waiting for a revolution to take place, claiming to be cooks for the mine — I don't think I'd care to partake of the table they laid out. Then there is a deputy U.S. marshal —"

"Marshal Turnbough seems like a very nice man," she said in his defense. "I think he's lonely, that's all, and I am an excellent judge of character, Mr. Mandell. I am sure the man is just shy." She paused. "And as for the Mexicans — I don't know."

"I don't either, but I'd like to find out."

"Why?"

"Curiosity. Wouldn't you care to know their true purposes?"

Rose hesitated. "I hadn't thought of it, but . . . yes, I suppose I would. I too am doubtful those three are only cooks." Her eyes flashed up, looked intently at him, as if trying to peer through murky water. "I am surprised that a man like you should have such a suspicious nature."

"A man like me?"

"I would have thought your brain would be filled with plans for the future of the mine. Things like the latest smelting techniques, tunnels, flumes, and tramways . . . or perhaps contemplating the complexities of mining law, like all these legal haggles I read about over the Apex law." She paused to study him, then glanced into the blackness beyond the railing. In the moonlight the high bluffs across the river appeared as heaps of bleached bones. "What do you think of the Apex law, Mr. Mandell?" she asked him quite unexpectedly.

The suddenness of it caught him with his thoughts elsewhere. "The what . . . ?" He stopped himself. "Er, what I mean is, I think they serve their purpose just fine."

She gave him a curious look, then smiled charmingly, like a perfectly rendered portrait. "I'm sorry. I don't know how my mind works sometimes, leaping from one thing to the next."

"We were talking about Edwardo, and Felix, and Ramon," he reminded her.

"Of course we were."

Somewhere along the line the detective had given over the direction of the conversation. Now he grabbed the reins and hauled it away from the uncomfortable ground it had begun to tread. "Anyway, as I was saying, you picked a fine boat for your first taste of adventure away from home, Miss Haven."

"I do see your point," she said.

Turnbough came up the gallery from back by the paddle wheel. He halted at Rose's side and said, "I should have thought you'd been asleep by now, Miss Haven." He glanced sternly at Mandell then back to Rose.

"I shall, in a little while. The evening was

pleasant, and Mr. Mandell thought it would be a shame to not enjoy some of it."

"He did?"

Mandell said, "How are you feeling, Marshal?"

"How I feel is none of your concern." Open challenge was in the marshal's eye.

Rose looked a bit startled at his rebuke.

Turnbough said to her, "Would you do the honor of accompanying me on a turn about the boat before you retire, Miss Haven?"

A moment of confusion registered on her lovely face. She glanced at Mandell.

He gave her a smile that seemed to ease the conflict suddenly pulling at her, and said, "I am certain the marshal will see you safely to your quarters afterward. I think it is time for me to turn in anyway."

In a glance, challenges were exchanged between the two men. Mandell allowed the edge of a grin to show, then returned his view to Rose. "I'll see you in the morning.

"Good night, then."

"Good night," she said.

Mandell put his back to Turnbough and strolled forward where the shadows lay heavy. Hidden, he paused to glance down the gallery. Rose and Turnbough moved from the railing and began a leisurely tour around the dark boat. Although he now knew a darker side to this man, he suspected that Rose was in no danger. Yet a suddenly rising ire toward Turnbough made the Pinkerton detective want to keep an eye on him.

He rejected that notion, if only because it would have been unfair to Rose to follow their progress around the deck.

Chan Loo had set up the cots earlier. Gilligan McPeevy was already sound asleep in one of them, snoring softly, irregularly. At his side was the lump of dark tubes and tartan cloth, looking vaguely like an octopus out of water. Mandell shucked his jacket and tucked his shoulder holster with the .38 Lightning among its folds. He shoved it under one of the cots, noting that four were unoccupied. The Mexicans were off somewhere. Perhaps spending the night ashore with the crew. He knew Turnbough's location, heard the man's heavy boots on the gallery beyond the wall and the ringing pleasant sound of Rose's laugh.

An uneasiness settled like a bag of coins upon his chest as he stretched to gaze up at the ceiling. An uneasiness born not so much from concern for Rose's safety as for his own desire to be the one strolling the deck at her side tonight — not Turnbough. He dismissed the sudden overwhelming anger, put its fire completely out — drowned it beneath a bucket of cold water called reason. He had settled this question years ago. So long as he worked for Allan Pinkerton, there was no room in his life for a wife and family.

Mandell closed his eyes, distantly aware of the muted sounds of sleeping people beyond the curtain on the far side of the cabin, and went to sleep.

17

Turnbough brought Rose Haven around to the back door of the main cabin, told her good night, and waited as she slipped into the dark room.

"Good night," she responded pleasantly, then promised a stroll the evening next. As she closed the door behind her, her brain was muddled and her emotions surging. Her thoughts immediately shifted from the marshal to Harrison Mandell.

He was certainly different.

Rose Haven had not known very many men socially — a father, brother, and four male cousins didn't count in matters like this — and the few men she had known were nothing at all like Harrison Mandell. Mandell was clearly good-looking — in a rugged way that somehow clashed with the stylish clothes. But that wasn't it. There was a quiet self-assuredness about him. Well, a man who has traveled the country, the world for that matter, would know how to handle himself . . . yet she had sensed something else, a timidness that lurked in that forest of strength, as if he could handle other men with impunity, but women were an area he had not quite fully explored.

Yes, maybe that, she decided.

She peered around the dark quarters, seeing the shapes of Molly and her girls on the cots placed about.

I'm finally out on my own.

She discovered she was suddenly standing a little taller — not that she ever had problems in that area. She had acquired her father's height, and his persistence. From her mother — her eyes and, thank goodness, her nose as well.

All at once Rose Haven was smiling.

She really was on her own now, *and not doing such a bad job of it!* She thought back to that first night, and dinner with Harrison Mandell in the Southern Pacific Hotel dining room. Miss Filvia would have been proud. Knives and forks all properly employed. Elbows firmly but comfortably at her sides. *Spine like a fencepost!* The words came back to her and brought a smirk to her lips. How she had hated those drills. Just the same, Miss Filvia knew what she was talking about.

What would Miss Filvia have thought of Mr. Mandell? If asked, she would have given the question careful consideration, poised like a beached whale in lavender and smelling of lilac water; her feet properly positioned, her hands folded one atop the other in front of her, her posture correct to the point of being positively painful to watch. Miss Filvia would have cleared her throat, only once, making it sound a little like a stifled cough, and begun to expound on his strong traits, making it perfectly clear, by omission, what his negative traits were. She would have most certainly noticed his eyes and the peculiar way they dissected whatever it was they were observing, as if somewhere in it lay a secret hidden from casual attention. But would Miss Filvia have mentioned them? Rose herself did not know how she felt about his curious form of scrutiny.

Well, that was a matter to be considered later — if later should prove to find him more involved in her life. For now, one step at a time. Here she was on her way. A bit more than a hundred miles by boat from her final destination; a whole new life in a new world. And Mr. Mandell would occupy only a small part of it for the next few months, and then who knows where in the world his company would send him next? . . . Odd, he hadn't mentioned the name of his company. Come to think of it, he hadn't spoken much about himself at all, and instead skillfully turned every conversation back to her, drawing out her life's story like a loose end of yarn from a garment, one knot at a time. And there were the other things too; things she found curious for a man whose life revolved around mining. . . .

Well, Mr. Mandell, two can play that game, she told herself, feeling very clever, and happy, and a little self-assured too. She was twenty-three, after all. About time to be on her own.

On the other side of the curtain, Rose heard Turnbough's footsteps and the door close. A window was raised. A bottle clinked against glass. The sounds filled her brain with visions, and she chided herself for being so easily infected with Mandell's suspicions. Yet there was a certain allure in the unknown, in a mystery — even if it was only a puzzle conjured up in one's own head, having no grounding in real life. The Mexicans were, in fact, probably exactly what they claimed. She glanced at Darlinda in the dark. Could she help it if one of the natives found the color of her hair curious? And the captain. A lot of men disliked their jobs. There was nothing startling or sinister in that. Yet Mandell seemed to think so. And what was it he was trying to hint at about Marshal Turnbough anyway?

Turnbough had been the perfect gentleman, had talked about his life back east and coming west for his health. He seemed to like his job now. One of many he had held. A coach driver for a Missouri line. A smithy's apprentice. A stevedore for the Keokuck and St. Louis Packet Company — come to think, Turnbough had been far more open with her than had Mandell.

She sat on one of the cots, but the pace of her thoughts precluded sleep, and she stood at once and quietly opened the back door. Stars swept across the sky, clear and bright. The desert air was cool and clean at this late hour.

Above her, on the hurricane deck, low-spoken words drifted down. Rose paid them no mind at first, until she realized that what she was hearing was a quiet conversation being carried out in Spanish. For an instant her thoughts went back to San Francisco, and in a dreamlike way to Pedro Montoya in the darkness of her father's barns, explaining to her in Spanish the intricacies of caring for a stableful of Thoroughbreds. Pedro had never learned to speak English, and had delighted at instructing the young *señorita* in the language of his country.

The pleasant memory faded. It took only a moment for Rose to comprehend the nature of this conversation. And once she did, she backed quietly up against the wall of the main cabin so that she could not be seen from above.

"I do not trust these North Americans." She recognized Ramon's voice, his short laugh, heard the quiet scrape of boots upon the deck as they shifted position. "Diego and the others, they should be above the Narrows by now. What do you think, Felix?"

"I think you worry too much, Ramon."

"You should be worried too. This far north into a foreign country with so many soldiers around would make any man worry."

Rose could hear the sound of a drink being taken, and then a satisfied sigh, and Felix's voice. "I think it is more than only that, my friend."

Ramon did not reply, and Rose imagined the man's frowning face staring off into the night.

Felix went on, and as he spoke the scuff of their boots carried the voices away. "If Carlos was my brother in the jail of the Yankee soldiers — ah, well, do not worry, my friend. Every man who has come up with us knows the importance of the revolution . . ." The voices faded into the night, replaced by the creaks and groans of the boat tugged gently against her moorings.

What had she heard? Really, only enough to pique her curiosity. She was confused, and tired — too tired to figure it out right now. Mandell's suspicious nature was absolutely infectious, she chided herself, and stepped back inside the cabin and went to bed.

18

The cargo hold of the *Bad Water* sweltered in the summer heat like the inside of a coking oven. Mandell had no firsthand knowledge of what coking ovens might be like, but he had read a description of one in *Fulbright's*, and the analogy seemed somehow appropriate now. The fine cracks in the decking a few inches above his head allowed in long, dusty threads of sunlight that traced ruler-straight lines on the wooden planks beneath his hands and knees and up and down the topography of crates of cargo stacked about. But the cracks did little to release the trapped heat.

Mandell started aft, hearing the bang of footsteps on the main deck overhead and the voices of men going about the business of operating a steamboat. All at once the hatchway he had just entered lifted. He wheeled about. Hunched down there in the cramped space he saw the square of light opening up, and Rose's face appear. She smiled at him.

"Good morning, Mr. Mandell," she said, and the next moment the opening was filled with her skirt as she dropped lightly down beside him.

"What are you doing here?"

She closed the hatch and looked back at him. "I might ask you the same question."

"I'm . . . I'm . . . I'm exploring."

"Then I will explore with you," she said happily. "What are we exploring for?" Her voice had lowered conspiratorially.

The rhythm of the steam engine pounded through the vessel, up his arms and along his thighs as he hunkered there seeing her half-mocking smile. He immediately considered abandoning the plan, but Rose Haven was a clever woman, and she would never allow him a moment from her sight if he didn't satisfy at least part of her curiosity. Perhaps he could still salvage something of his cover afterward. He said, "Last night Chan came down here, apparently at the captain's bidding. It was too dark to see what he was up to, but he acted suspicious enough to tickle my curiosity."

Rose looked disappointed. "Oh, only that. I thought perhaps you had discovered the Mexicans' true purposes, or some other nefarious plot afoot."

He frowned. "Down here?"

She smiled innocently. "It does not seem to be any more farfetched than suspecting Chan's business last night was anything more than boat related. After all, the captain did order it. You said so yourself."

He sat back and looked at her in the dusty

ribbons of light. "You know, Miss Haven, you have a knack for ruining a perfectly good mystery."

"Please, call me Rose."

He hitched up an eyebrow. That, at least, was a small step forward in their association.

"Well?" she said. "It's awful hot down here. Suppose we get on with it?"

"Yes, ma'am." He started toward the aft of the boat with Rose at his heels. Three-quarters of the way back he encountered the lantern Chan had used the night before, resting in a box attached to one of the vertical deck supports.

The detective crept on and said to Rose, "I don't know exactly what I'm looking for, except that I had the impression last night that Chan had opened a cabinet, or cupboard. Whatever, it definitely had a metal latch. I heard that plain enough."

"That should not be so hard to find," she said behind him. "So far the only things we have encountered are crates — nothing resembling a cabinet."

"Whatever it was, it was beyond that lantern we just passed."

He was below the cabins now. The lines of light overhead had ceased abruptly. He was beginning to wonder if Chan had gone this far back. In the blackness of the previous night it was impossible to judge distance. Mandell paused among the crates to look around.

He slapped his arm and grinned wryly at the spot of blood. "Even down in this inferno there's no relief from the persistent buggers."

Rose smirked.

In the dim half-light one crate looked like another, and none of them looked like a cupboard. He studied the open curved beams of the hull. Last night he had the impression of ribs as Chan's light had flashed over them, and now, seeing them again, he recalled an amusing story he'd read — probably during one of his long and all-too-frequent train trips — of a wooden puppet swallowed up by a whale.

He put his wandering thoughts back on the job before him, padding hand over hand, deeper into the bowels of the *Bad Water*, stopping here and there to examine a suspicious box or crate, inspecting the walls and supports, looking for anything resembling a cupboard. Sweat spilled from his head. The heat was like a hundredweight upon his shoulders. After a while he crawled up to a wall and leaned back against it. Rose had wilted. Hair limp. Cheeks glistening.

"Give up?" she asked, employing her handkerchief. The effort didn't help much.

"Not yet." His thoughts seemed suddenly to be drawn to the cool mountains of Colorado that he had known, and try as he might, he could not pull them back. He wondered vaguely if the heat had not begun to addle his brain. He was thinking about that beer again — what had it been called? Its name had been the same as the German who brewed it. Leaning there, gathering in the loose ends of his thoughts that seemed bent on unraveling, he imagined he could hear the gurgle of a Rocky Mountain stream — but it was only the water under the keel.

Or was it?

He sat up straight.

"What is it?" Rose asked, concerned by his suddenness.

The sound diminished to a faint rushing current — a slightly different frequency from the river churning below the hull.

"Do you hear that?"

"What?" Her eyes took on an intense scowl.

He leaned back against the wall and the sound increased. When he put his ear to it, the rushing of running water came through clearly.

"On the other side of this." His muddled brain sharpened and he forgot the heat. A crazy thought suddenly occurred to the detective as he recalled Chan Loo's trick with the mason jar kept cool at the end of a rope.

Rose listened against the wall. Her scowl widened to puzzlement. "What does it mean?"

He scrambled around the wall, and as he suspected, it turned out to be not a wall at all, but a box built from floor to low ceiling, a bit more than an arm's span to a side. A couple of raps convinced him it was sturdily built. On one of the four sides he came to a halt at a heavy, nickel-plated latch with the name WHITE CLAD cast into it, provided with an equally heavy padlock to keep the tightly fitted door firmly shut.

An icebox latch!

Mandell tugged at the lock, then fished a leather folder from his pocket.

"What is that?"

"You don't see this," he said, and in the poor light selected a thin steel pick and inserted it into the keyhole. In a moment the lock clicked and came apart. Mandell put away his tools.

"Is that what they teach at the Colorado School of Mines these days?"

"You would be simply amazed at the liberal education offered nowadays," he said wryly. Talking his way out of this one was going to require some fancy verbal footwork, but that was something he could handle later. "I'll tell you all about it sometime," he said, and pulled the door open.

It was a heavy thing. A good four inches thick and full of insulation. A rush of cold air spilled out as the door widened. The inside of the box was too dark to make out, but this time he had remembered to bring matches along. He unscrewed the cap of a metal cylinder, withdrew one, struck it on the roughened side of the cylinder. Flame flared and Mandell thrust it inside.

Rose's head and his collided in the doorway.

Copper tubes ran up and down the sides and back of the box, attached all together at the bottom by a pipe fitting that looked to be a plumber's nightmare. The rush of river water through them wasn't quite like the sound of a Colorado mountain stream, but the difference was hardly worth mentioning.

The box was filled with bottles. Beer bottles! And in the middle of them was a wooden beer keg that had not yet been tapped. As the match burned near to his fingertips, Rose said she wondered if there was anything behind the keg, and gave it a shove. It tipped easily and she pushed it aside, but there was nothing but more copper tubing. Mandell held the match nearer to the cask . . .

Suddenly he remembered the name of that Colorado beer and the German who brewed it. It was the same as the name that was burned into the keg.

ADOLPH COORS.

The match nipped his fingertips and he shook it out. Darkness returned to the cool box. Mandell closed the door, relocked the latch, and crawled a few feet away to the side of the boat where he paused to think . . . and to open the wire stoppers on the two cold bottles in his hand.

19

"Well, there certainly is nothing illegal, immoral, or unhealthy about providing your own private cache of beer and keeping it a family secret. Especially in an inhospitable place like the Colorado River . . . but it does paint a somewhat disreputable picture of a captain who would flatly lie and proclaim there was no beer on board!" Mandell grinned wryly to himself in the gloom of the *Bad Water*'s cargo hold, relishing the condensing moisture in his fist, rolling the cool bottle across his forehead.

"But there is something illegal, immoral, and possibly unhealthy about picking the lock on another man's icebox and stealing his beer," Rose pointed out reasonably.

"Well, perhaps," Mandell said. But it didn't seem to diminish Rose's zeal for the cold drink right at the moment. His life these last twelve years would never bear up well under close scrutiny. Allan was not one to look too closely at how his "operatives" — as he preferred to call the detectives who worked for him — carried out their jobs, so long as the results were satisfactory.

Still, Mandell could not quite decide how this discovery had any bearing on missing postal money orders that he had been sent to find. But that was a minor difficulty, and it did not subtract from the wonderful taste of the beer.

He came out of his reverie all at once. The forward hatch had swung open. Rose looked at him, startled. He put a finger to his lips. Someone had entered the hold, and now that someone was making a scraping, rattling sound, working his way back toward them. Mandell finished the beer quickly and set the bottle quietly aside.

He thought of Chan Loo at first, and wondered if the Chinese man was coming back for another nip. Then a pair of voices reached him over the pounding of the steam engines overhead.

"*Estamos cerca de la quilla,*" Edwardo said to someone nearby.

Mandell eased forward and found a place behind the crates where he could view the two Mexicans working their way down the center aisle. Rose crawled up beside him.

"*¿Pero que buscamos?*" Ramon asked, looking perplexed, and miserably hot in his hat, jacket, and heavy ornate gun belt.

Edwardo shrugged his shoulders. "*¡Como se yo!*"

"*Si tu no sabes. ¿Como los vamos a encontrar?*"

Mandell frowned. He glanced at Rose recalling that she had said she spoke the language. "Do you understand what they are saying?" he whispered near her ear.

"*Callaté y continua buscando,*" Edwardo said. Even though Mandell could not understand the words, the bandit's impatience was plain.

Rose said softly, "They seem to be searching for something, but they don't know what."

"*Quizas este debajo del cargo.*"

"*Si tenemos que mover el cargo lo moveremos.*"

Rose whispered, "They are looking for something that might be under the cargo. Edwardo says if they have to, they will move the cargo."

Ramon frowned. The Mexican glanced along the floor and his view stopped on something. He rapped the floor with his knuckles. "*Aqui esta un escotillón.*"

Edwardo broke off his search immediately and lent a hand. Together they lifted out a section in the floor and both heads came together over the opening.

"*¡Este es!*" Edwardo said, excited.

"They seem to have found what they are looking for," Rose said quietly.

"*Tenemos que buscar los otros. Uno no es sufficiente.*"

"They want to find another. Apparently one will not be enough," she translated freely at his side.

"Another what?"

Rose shook her head. "No idea yet."

Ramon looked around and shrugged his shoulders. The two men replaced the section and continued investigating the cracks in the floor. As they drew nearer to Mandell's position, the detective made no movement and quieted his breathing even though he was certain there was no way the Mexicans could hear breathing over the constant *chukety pow, chukety pow, chukety pow* of the steam engines overhead. And in the gloom and diffused light, they'd have to practically stumble over Rose and him to discover their hiding place. Just the same, he remained perfectly still.

"*¿Nada todavia?*"

"*No*," Ramon replied.

They were too close now for Rose to risk further translation. She lay dead still, her brown eyes big and round.

Mandell had a queer feeling in his stomach. A movement in his gut. And all at once he knew what the beer was doing to him.

The Mexicans drew up and studied the floor a while. Then they resumed their systematic search for . . . what was it they were looking for?

The gas bubble became painful. Mandell buried his mouth in his fist and allowed a small belch to escape. It made no noise, but at once the cargo hold was filled with the aroma of beer.

Ramon stopped and sniffed the air. He grinned and turned to Edwardo. *"Daria todo por una cerveza fria."*

Edwardo laughed. *"¡Estas loco! Has estado debajo del sol por demasiada tiempo, amigo. No vamos a encontrar ninguna cerveza fria en cien kilometros . . . quizas en mil kilometros."*

"Yo sé." Ramon looked pensive. *"¿Porque habre deseado una cerveza?"*

"Olvidalo. Sigue buscando." Edwardo's words cut short and he suddenly began shoving crates aside. One of them slammed into Mandell's shin, and when it hung up, Edwardo gave it a harder shove. *"Aqui. ¡Lo encontré!"* The two Mexicans hauled up another square of floor and peered into the black opening.

Grinning, Ramon thrust a triumphant fist in the air. The bandits returned the panel and spoke more words Mandell could not understand. Another knot had begun to tighten in his stomach, and the gas began to work its way up.

The Mexicans retreated toward the bow hatch. Mandell buried his mouth in both fists to stifle the belch that erupted forth, muffled, but still loud enough to hear.

He froze and waited.

Chukety pow, chukety pow, chukety pow . . .

The Mexicans lifted the hatch a fraction, peered through the crack, then flung it wide and scrambled outside.

It slammed shut, and Mandell relaxed,

belching without reserve. "Excuse me, Rose," he said, feeling better as he sat up to rub the tender spot on his shin.

"Quite understandable."

They crawled to the trapdoor and together pulled it up and out of the way. At the bottom of the black opening, an arm's length below, was a big iron plug with an iron ring welded to its top, set into a metal fitting on the hull of the boat.

The detective's face came up wearing a perplexed look.

"What is it?" Rose asked him.

"It's a bilge plug."

"What's a bilge plug?"

"It can be opened to drain out water that gathers in the bottom of a boat."

"What interest could those men have in the boat's bilge plug?"

"Good question." He replaced the door, crawled forward to examine the other opening the Mexicans had discovered. The result was the same.

Mandell scowled into the hazy gloom, considering. "One thing is certain, these three are not cooks — although it is apparently clear they are cooking up something here aboard the *Bad Water*."

Rose said, "That was what I wanted to tell you when I followed you here. Last night I overheard them talking about it."

"And?"

"I didn't catch all of it, but apparently there are others waiting for them upriver, at a place they called the Narrows. They also said something about someone being held in jail by the cavalry."

"Go on," he prodded when she fell silent.

Rose shrugged her shoulders. "That's all there is. I didn't hear any more. They had moved off by that time."

"Too bad." He gazed at the dusty shafts of light coming through the floorboards overhead without really seeing them. The last thing he needed was another puzzle. He had plenty enough to work on already.

20

The *Bad Water* ran aground for the second time at precisely eleven twenty-four. Mandell knew the hour because he had just emerged from the bow hatch and was looking at his watch when the boat struck, jolting him and Rose up against the railing as it ground to a halt on a rocky shoal. For a few moments the big paddle wheel continued to turn, throwing up a foam, not moving the boat anywhere, and then it too stopped.

Mandell shoved the watch into his pocket. "Are you all right?"

Rose nodded her head and brushed ineffectively at the dusty brown dress. It was showing the strain of the trip and would require more than a superficial brushing to get it back in shape. "Yes. I am quite all right."

"I best see if I can help," he said then, and joined the men who had snatched up poles and were running them into the water. He took up a pole, and as the paddle wheel started in reverse, the detective glanced at the bluffs above the river. They were there again, laughing. The old chief, his son, and all the rest of the Quechans. Mandell thought of Tommy Morgan up in the wheelhouse. The pilot's face would be glowing about this time. Well, it was hardly his fault, Mandell allowed. This river had a reputation for catching boats. They spent almost as much time stuck on sandbars as they spent in open water.

A bell clanged, the engines stopped, and Patronoff showed up; first to study the situation, and then to climb the stairs to the wheelhouse and confer with his pilot.

Rose Haven shaded her eyes and bent over the railing to peer at the bow slanted up out of the water.

"You better keep back, miss," one of the hands warned, his sweating shoulders bulging as he strained at the poles.

Rose found a place by the railing and clasped it as if at any moment expecting another jolt from the grounded vessel. Molly and her girls appeared shortly, and the marshal too. Turnbough said something to Darlinda. They both laughed and she threaded an arm through his. Mandell saw the pinched look that came to Rose's face. Up on the boiler deck, McPeevy was peering down, and his concern seemed to be on something other than the boat having run aground again. As the Scotsman absentmindedly stroked the big cat in his arms behind the ears, his attention remained pointedly directed at Darlinda and the marshal.

From two decks above, Patronoff barked down to them. "Hold up there, boys. We are goin' to try an' grasshopper her over this one."

"Grasshoppering" was something Mandell had read about — probably in a Pullman car somewhere — and he was curious to see exactly how it was accomplished. He climbed the stairs to the boiler deck where McPeevy was standing next to the railing.

The Scotsman came out of his thoughts, smiled pleasantly at him. "I du'na think we will reach the Bad Water Mine any time soon — not if Mr. Morgan keeps running us up on the shoals."

"It's not his fault. Besides, it does prevent the trip from becoming humdrum."

McPeevy grinned. "Aye, that it does."

Mandell indicated the bow where men were busy unlashing lines. "This should prove interesting."

McPeevy glanced at the men — out of politeness, the detective thought. Mostly the Scotsman looked bored with the whole affair.

The deckhands were maneuvering a pair of long wooden spars, attached to the tops of two tall derricks, into the river. With the two spars firmly embedded into the river bottom on either side of the bow, ropes were spun around steam capstans at the bow and a small engine began to chug, drawing in the line, pulling back on the heavy spars.

The spars bit deep into the muddy bottom, pulled back, and with a shudder the *Bad Water* crept forward a few feet and stopped. The spars were pulled up then, and the crew repeated the process, each time gaining a few feet. In half an hour the steamboat had pulled itself over the shoal and was floating clear of it again.

Patronoff ordered the boat hove along shore for a complete inspection of the paddle wheel, which had grated hard upon the bottom of the river as they had grasshoppered over.

"This can take a few hours," he informed the passengers who gathered on the main deck. He inclined his great, bearded head at the bank of the river where they had come to land. A small canyon worked its way back into the bluffs, and a trickle of water issuing from it increased in its own small way the volume that eventually flowed into the Gulf of California. "There are trees for shade, and fresh water, it appears. You might want to disembark and stretch your legs while we check over the boat."

Darlinda at once shook her head. "Ain't no way I'm going to go ashore, not with those crazy Indians about!"

"I will keep an eye on you, miss," Mandell offered, and observed out the corner of his eye a quick, disapproving glance from Rose. "Although," he continued, "it appears our

Indian friends have departed."

"Thanks, but no thanks," she said. "I intend to keep my hindquarters right here where I can find a door real quick to hide behind."

Edwardo gave her a grin. "The Indians, they will not bother you, *señorita*. I make you that promise." He sounded quite confident, Mandell thought. He was, after all, well armed. "Yumans are not warriors. They are *muy* friendly."

"Too friendly for my liking," Darlinda shot back.

"I will remain aboard with you," Marshal Turnbough said.

"No! . . . I mean, you don't have to. I will be perfectly all right. Besides, I like being alone sometimes."

Gangplank was swung over the gunwales and they disembarked. Loo Han Ling carried a large wicker basket filled with sandwiches and fruit. Felix came from the main cabin with a bottle of tequila in his fist.

Mandell put himself in Rose's way. "May I assist, Miss Haven — Rose?" he asked, offering an arm.

"Thank you," she said coolly, and lifted the hem of her skirt, stepping onto the gangplank.

The marshal, Mandell noted, had remained on the boat despite Darlinda's request to be left alone. He was watching

Chan Loo shinnying along the connecting rod to examine its attachment point on the great wheel, but the detective suspected Turnbough's true interest was in a certain redheaded woman now ascending the steps toward the main cabin.

They hiked up the stream a few hundred feet where the evil sun could not reach them. The air remained stifling hot and humid, and swarms of black gnats followed them from the river. Molly and Betty found a place to sit down, and immediately dragged their skirts up above their knees and began to fan their calves. Rose averted her eyes, embarrassed. Loo Han Ling searched for a place to lay out lunch. McPeevy continued a few feet farther up the stream and dropped King Robert the Second to the ground. The cat went down to the water for a drink, then curled up in the shade to implement a thorough cleanup job on his legs, stomach, and tail.

Edwardo and Felix hovered over the basket as Loo Han Ling unloaded it onto a blue tablecloth spread out on the ground. Ramon, the detective observed, had stayed aboard the *Bad Water*. They were being subtle about it, taking their leave in shifts. Mandell frowned. What the devil were they up to? Rose abandoned his arm to lend a hand laying out lunch.

Turnbough came along later, a curiously pleased grin on his healing face. He snatched up a handful of sandwiches and some tea Loo Han Ling had brought along in a widemouth mason jar, and carried them off a ways to devour undisturbed.

After they all had eaten their fill, Rose and Loo Han Ling covered the remaining food with a cotton napkin and took off together on a stroll up the stream. Mandell kept an eye on the two women until a bend put them out of sight. He finished his second sandwich and stood, stretched, and wandered back to the boat to see how the inspection was going. The mournful sound of bagpipes turned him aside. He found a flat rock next to McPeevy and sat down.

McPeevy played on for some time, the music both foreign and restful. The final tune ended, dying away as the bag deflated, and McPeevy looked over and asked an odd question. "What do ye think of coincidences?"

Mandell had been fingering up a rock to toss at the stream. The music, strangely soothing, had given his brain an opportunity to hoe around the puzzles that had sprouted since this trip had begun. He looked over at the Scotsman and made a face not quite a frown. "They happen from time to time, although not too frequently — at least not without help. I've known one or two coincidences that would not have been believed if written down in a book."

"Aye," McPeevy said with feeling, "so have I."

"You have yourself a coincidence?" Mandell asked neutrally.

McPeevy started to speak, then closed his mouth, and shook his head. "Nae. I du'na know what I was thinking about. Idle chatter, I suspect." He squinted at the hot blue sky through the dusty leaves of a cottonwood tree. "The sun, she fries a man's brain, addles it sure enough."

Captain Patronoff came up the trail from the river along with his men, and Darlinda and Ramon with them too, looking heat-weary, searching for a splash of shade to rest in, and something cold to drink, Mandell suspected. They trudged up the incline — haggard, every one of them, attacked the remaining sandwiches and finished up the tea, dropping about beneath the trees like half-filled sacks of sand.

"How did the inspection go?" Mandell asked.

Patronoff glanced over, his black beard unable to hide the sunburned cheeks, or the look of irritation in his eyes. "We lost some of the paddle boards on that one. Too damned hot now to do anything about it." He glowered at the sky. "We'll get to replacing them in a while."

McPeevy looked over and grinned resignedly. "What did I tell ye? It'll be days before we reach the mine."

Mandell too felt a weighty despair in the way things were going. "Days?" he said. "At this rate we might never reach it."

"We should have rented us those horses like we talked about," McPeevy said wistfully.

Mandell watched the Mexicans step off a few dozen paces and fall into serious talk. Once in a while a face would flash in their direction. This delay was definitely not in their plans. If only he knew what those plans were, one of his puzzles could be put away. But then what would he do when he retired them all? His brain thrived on conundrums. Well, he grinned wryly to himself, he'd just have to find something new to work on.

His thought came to a halt. A woman's cry had echoed suddenly down the canyon — Rose's cry!

21

His immediate thought was that the Quechans had returned. That same worry must have been on the minds of each of them because the detective noted more than a few revolvers appearing as the men leaped to their feet. But it became apparent a moment later that Rose's cries were not from distress but excitement.

She hurried down the trail a few yards until in plain sight, stopped, and gave a huge beckoning wave of her arm. Once she had their attention and knew they understood, she turned back, grabbing up her skirts, and led the way.

They all clamored up the trail. She had piqued their curiosity right enough, and as weapons disappeared back into various holsters and waistbands, the small band wondered what had happened. Even Molly and her girls joined in, and the Mexicans too, chattering away in Spanish. The detective half wished Rose had remained to translate for him.

Around the bend Mandell spied Rose and Loo Han Ling ahead on hands and knees, examining something half protruding from the base of the cliff. He and Patronoff arrived first, mainly because they had been nearest when Rose had riveted their attentions.

"What in blazes is so important —" Patronoff started to say as he strode the last few paces. His words ended abruptly.

Mandell stepped ahead and bent near to the object Rose was indicating. It was a curved piece of thin steel, dimpled, as if hammered in shape, and engraved along the edges. The women had cleared only a small portion of it, but its shape was immediately recognized, and in a rush both men dropped to their knees and began digging the rest of it out.

By the time the others arrived, they had wrenched it free of the red sand and were brushing the last of the sand off it.

"What have you?" Edwardo asked, shouldering through the knot of people.

"Would you look at this?" Patronoff bellowed, amazed and intrigued at the same time. Except for a few leather straps mostly rotted off save for a few rivets and buckles, the rest of it was in perfect condition. As shiny in places as when it had left the armory in Spain. Patronoff hauled it around where the sun caught the metal — perhaps for the first time in 350 years.

"Conquistadors!" he said, holding the steel

breastplate high above his head as if it were a prize hard won.

"It would have had to have been lost in the 1500s," Rose said. "Isn't it a wonderful find?"

"What's it worth?" Molly asked pragmatically. She sounded singularly disappointed, and looked put out at having made the climb for this.

"Worth?" Rose was stunned. "You mean money? In dollars, probably very little, but as an archaeological find it is extremely valuable."

Ramon stepped off a few feet and began scanning the ground where hardy cactus clung to bits of windswept rocks.

"Honey, if you can't spend it, eat it, wear it . . ." She eyed the bit of armor. "Well, I reckon in some circles it may have been fashionable attire — it ain't worth old beans." She started back down. "Come on along, girls."

But Darlinda and Betty hung back, curious.

Molly huffed and departed. Ramon's shout brought a halt to her steps and turned her around, but she did so not wanting her inquisitiveness to show through the curtain of practicality she had just raised.

Ramon fell to his knees and in a moment was shaking the sand out of a steel helmet — and something fell out of it.

A white skull clunked to the ground, rolled

over, and stopped against a stone, empty eye sockets staring up at them.

"Looks like we found the other part of him," Mandell said, hefting the skull. "Probably scattered by coyotes when he died."

"I wonder how he died," Darlinda said in a tone that displayed more than mere curiosity, almost an intense morbid interest.

"Maybe Indians," Mandell suggested.

This did not sit well with her, and immediately Darlinda turned her attention to the high bluffs overhead. Meanwhile, the crew had begun kicking around the site. McPeevy put aside his bagpipes to help and King Robert the Second curled up on the tartan bag to watch him.

It was Turnbough who made the next discovery: a leg bone that he wrestled from the ground and waved over his head. Digging around it, Alf Danderfault came up with a stirrup and some pieces of leather still intact, and started in on a story about a dead man he'd found frozen in the ice while hunting polar fox in the Kjölen Mountains in Norway.

Chan Loo found the second skull. This gave rise to a sudden excitement. There was more than one man buried here! Patronoff told one of the deckhands to run back to the *Bad Water* for shovels and picks.

Betty wondered if it wasn't bad luck to go digging them up like that — disrespectful.

But no one paid her any mind as they pulled armor and short swords from the ground, having a good time at it.

Mandell climbed a pile of rocks and noted the position of each find. It became clear after half a dozen more unearthings that what they had here was the dying grounds of at least six men and perhaps twice that many horses.

Then Loo Han Ling made the discovery that compelled even Molly into the mad fray to turn over ground. What Chan's wife discovered fit Molly's narrow criteria as to what was valuable. It came out of the soil as only a heavy wooden box fitted with steel hinges. But when Felix's shovel crashed down upon it and gold doubloons spilled out across the ground, the good-natured hunt roiled immediately into a frenzy.

The heat was forgotten and the afternoon flew by. No further thought was given to the damaged steamboat, or the persistent Indians who had gathered on a ridge a few hundred yards away to watch the curious carryings on of these ambitious white people. Everyone lent a hand. Shovels threw off clouds of red dirt, picks dislodged rocks and bones. Everything went into piles: steel armor and weapons onto one, bones onto another, doubloons onto a third.

By nightfall the entire area had been turned upside-down. Exhausted, and delighted, the camaraderie was exemplary as they gathered up their booty and hauled it all down to the boat and up to the main cabin where the long table was immediately overwhelmed.

"It looks like a museum display," Rose said, standing back to note the items all lined up.

Mandell thought so too, but his attention was fixed on the pile of gold doubloons at the far end, and the way Ramon and Felix and Molly and the captain and Chan Loo were eyeing them too. In fact, everyone but Rose had an eye on the gold.

Rose seemed the only person there more interested in the archaeological significance of the find than what the pile would fetch when cashed in.

Mandell suddenly had a vision of circling vultures, and they all seemed to be circling each other.

22

"I say we split up the money, each of us gettin' our share of it," Molly proclaimed, making certain everyone understood that although she was all for ending the expedition before it began, once the true merit of the venture had been determined, she had been right there in the fray, getting her hands dirty with the rest of them.

"Aye! I concur. Let's split it now!" McPeevy seconded. He seemed to have developed a persistent itch on the palms of his hands.

There was a general agreement on this, but Chan Loo stood up and shook his head. "No — no splitee up now. Too many pilees to watchee. Bad man come, bang, bang on backee of head and stealee. No good, no good." He wagged his head emphatically. "Keepee all gold in one pilee. All keepee watchee until get to mine. Better idea. Yes, yes."

"What the hell is that Chinaman jabbering about now?" Molly demanded.

Chan spoke quickly to his wife. Loo Han Ling bobbed her head as he explained it to her. "My husband is afraid that if the money is split up now, each of us stands a greater chance of being robbed of our share."

Mandell did not think it intentional, yet he could not help notice that Loo Han Ling's eyes darted continually toward the three Mexicans as she spoke.

"Husband says money safer if kept in one place and guarded all times by three or four men."

"Men!" Molly roared. "I can damn well guard my own money as good as any man. Just give me a gun and I'll show you. And I can guard my share alone better than the whole pot!"

"We will guard our own money too," Edwardo put in, and Ramon and Felix at once agreed.

Quiet Betty suddenly spoke up. "I don't know that I like the idea of having all that money with me," she said. "I'm not very good with a gun, even if I had one. I think I would prefer to get my share at the end of the trip so that I can put it in a safe place right away." She looked around for support for her position.

McPeevy, after considering the logic of this, stood up on her side, and so did Darlinda, Loo Han Ling, Chan, and Rose — although Mandell suspected Rose's intentions were more along the line of keeping the discovery intact while she figured out a way to convince them to turn it all over to a museum. And she might also try convincing water to run uphill while she was at it, he mused.

The debate ended at that moment when a voice called out from on the shore. "Captain Patronoff," it said. "Ho, Captain! You in big boat?"

Darlinda's eyes bulged. "Oh, no!" she cried. "They're back!"

Everyone piled out of the cabin into the growing gloom of the approaching night.

Mandell found Darlinda standing at his side by the railing. The natural paleness of her cheeks had reddened dramatically — but the hue had nothing to do with fright, and everything to do with flat-out anger. Her fists clenched, teeth grating. "Will those damned savages never leave me alone? Oooo! What I wouldn't give for a gun . . . or a pint of strychnine." Suddenly she was grinning as if she contemplated something humorous, and she glanced wickedly at Mandell. "Or just leave me alone with that overstimulated savage half an hour with a good sharp knife, and I'll have some interesting baubles to hang from my coupstick."

Betty giggled softly into her hand. Molly said sternly, "You know you don't mean that, honey." She caught Darlinda's eye and shot a warning glance in Mandell's direction.

He pretended not to notice — but he did notice that McPeevy had remained inside the cabin. The Scotsman was busy stuffing something into the valise, and trying not to be obvious in the way his view kept shifting forward at — at himself? No. Mandell knew it was Darlinda again that he was watching. McPeevy gathered up the valise and carried it out the back door of the main cabin.

The Indians splashed into the water up to their knees and gathered around the bow of the boat. The old chief tried to maintain a bit of dignity, and approached on horseback.

Captain Patronoff halted at the main stairway and shouted to a deckhand below. "Hale up that gangplank, mister." He looked over at Darlinda. "You don't have to worry about them," he said. "I won't let 'em aboard, but if it makes you feel better, you can retreat to my cabin. There is a lock on the door." He fished a key from his vest pocket and handed it to Darlinda.

"Thank you, Captain," she said, gathering up her skirts and bustling away. Mandell caught a glimpse of her below, through the railing, and then she was gone, and Patronoff had resumed his determined march to the front of the boat. In his wake, the crew and most of the passengers tagged along.

The detective looked around for McPeevy, but the Scotsman had disappeared completely. Mandell descended the staircase along with the rest of them.

Angry words exploded like firecrackers in

the hot air. "I already told you, Chief," Patronoff growled with rising aggravation, "the woman ain't for sale!"

The chief was not going to be easily put off this time. "I give you two hundred dollar. Good money. Gold!"

Olley wasn't there, and that surprised the detective. Mandell shifted his view to the mud-painted face up on the shore and didn't find him there either. He turned an eye to the low brush growing in patches along the shore.

"Alf!" Patronoff barked, his patience fully run out. He shot a glance over his shoulder at the tall, sandy-haired fireman. "Go find me a gun!"

Alf Danderfault went off wearing a quizzical look, not sure if the captain was serious or only bluffing. And at the moment Mandell wasn't so certain either — but more important, neither was the old chief.

"Hokay, hokay, Captain," the chief said, patting the air placatingly. "I know I try to skin you alive." He grinned and his old face wrinkled like a prune. "Ho, you too smart for me. Hokay, hokay. I sweeten pot. How 'bout two fifty?"

"You best rouse yourselves out of here or I'm a-haling out my deck howitzer and blowing you and your flea-bitten menagerie to hell!"

"They won't have very far to go," Mandell

commented to Rose beneath his breath.

She looked over and smirked.

"Excuse me," he said, and made his way through the piles of cargo to the river side of the boat and down the port-side gallery. He paused a moment at the door of Captain Patronoff's cabin, heard no sound from beyond it. At the front of the boat the bartering and the threats continued, and he suspected that both men were rather enjoying the banter despite themselves. He continued on past the engine room where the wheel support stretched out over dark water behind the boat, stepped out onto it and across to one of the wide paddles, sliding up between the paddle wheel and rear of the engine room.

The bartering went on and on. The chief was not being put off, not even in the face of Patronoff's threat, but Mandell had begun to suspect that the old man had another game up his sleeve.

He came alert. Quiet footsteps padded the deck not so very far forward. He hadn't expected anyone from that direction. The crew and passengers were caught up in the carrying on between Patronoff and the old chief. A hinge squeaked — Mandell identified the sound as a deck hatch — and a word was spoken. It was only Chan Loo's soft singsong voice and Loo Han Ling's quiet reply . . . and then the deck hatch closed.

Mandell let out a breath, dismissed the two of them and returned his attention to the water, scanning the ripples moving in the evening twilight. After a few moments he began to wonder if he hadn't assumed wrongly.

There was a splash at the side.

Then another.

Mandell pressed up against the back of the boat.

A dripping hand reached up out of the water and latched onto the aft gunwale. A toe followed . . . a foot . . . a leg . . . an elbow . . . and finally Olley heaved himself full out of the river and stood on the deck, wary, dripping a puddle of water at his feet.

He appeared somehow different, and then Mandell knew why. The swim from the shore had washed most of the mud from his body. Clean — more or less — Olley wasn't such a bad-looking kid. Tall for an Indian, banded about the chest and shoulders with muscle.

Olley crouched quietly along the gallery, glancing into dark corners as he moved, pausing at the crew's storage room to peek inside. He closed the door quietly and went on to Chan Loo's quarters.

Mandell edged around the corner while Olley noiselessly closed the door to the Loos' room and stepped back to study the railing overhead on the boiler deck. He debated a moment, then, coming to a decision, shook his head and proceeded forward to Patronoff's cabin and tried the door.

When it didn't open, Olley rattled the handle again.

"Who's there?" Darlinda called softly, her voice tense.

Olley flashed a victorious grin and pulled at the knob with both hands.

"Go away whoever you are!"

Olley rammed a shoulder into the door. Wood creaked and Darlinda shrieked. Olley stepped back for another go at it.

"The lady asked you to go away," Mandell said amiably at his side.

Olley wheeled, startled, a wild-animal glare in his dark eyes.

The Pinkerton detective grinned back at the strapping lad.

The Indian gave no warning and lunged, closing strong fingers about Mandell's throat. He was powerful and immensely swift — both gifts of his youth and of his half-savage existence in the hostile deserts of southern Arizona. The attack drove Mandell up against the cabin wall.

Mandell gripped the Indian's wrists, realizing at once that his strength was no match for this young man. He drove up a knee, knocked the wind momentarily from the Indian, and at the same time twisted free. Gasping, he managed to sidestep Olley's next lunge, and was ready for him when he tried again, catching the young man below the ribs with bunched knuckles that folded him in two.

Olley staggered back, straightened, glanced at the locked door and the prize it protected, and in blind fury drove his attack forward. The force of it slammed the detective onto the deck, and only Mandell's streetwise instincts prevented Olley from latching onto his throat again. He managed to get a heel up as Olley dove forward and somersaulted the Indian over him. The kid landed on his back with a breath-wrenching thump.

Mandell had fallen across a hawser. He picked himself off of it painfully, aware that there were people at the far end of the boat, drawn by the sound of their fight.

Olley squirmed where he had landed but immediately was on his knees, and then he had his feet beneath him, resuming the attack. This time his intentions were clear. He was going to finish off the detective swiftly and steal away the woman before anyone could stop him. To that end he drew the long knife at his side.

Mandell slipped his right hand into his pocket. When it came out a brassy glint ringed his knuckles.

Olley lunged forward and the knife arced overhead, slicing empty air. Mandell jabbed up with a solid thrust to Olley's stomach that rattled the Indian's teeth.

Shock registered instantly on the young

man's face. A mere fist wasn't supposed to be that hard! Before he could figure it out, Mandell had come up again and connected — brass to chin.

Teeth crashed.

Bone crunched.

Blood filled his mouth and Olley staggered back and instantly collapsed.

Crew and passengers gathered around, along with a few of the Indians who had climbed aboard, suspecting the nature of the commotion.

The Quechans looked at Olley, glanced at Mandell, then back again, bewildered.

Patronoff forced his way through and peered down at the crumpled Indian. An amused look inched across his bearded face. He fished a cigar out of his shirt pocket and put a match to it.

"Well, well, well," Patronoff said around the cigar in his mouth. "We have us an uninvited guest." He glanced at Mandell. "You seem to have the situation under control right enough." Then he saw the knuckle dusters and the grin widened. "Throw the Indian overboard!"

Alf and Tommy Morgan moved in to do the honors. Mandell stepped aside for them, aware of the way Rose was watching him. He tried not to be obvious when he slipped his hand back into his pocket and brought it out again unadorned.

The Indians protested this rough treatment of their unconscious brother.

"I said throw the bastard overboard!" Patronoff rumbled, and the next moment Olley was describing a neat arc through the air. Two of the Quechans dove after the chief's son. Patronoff wheeled on the remaining Indians. "Get the hell off my boat! You bother us again, I'll use you for target practice!"

The report of a rifle brought their heads around. On the deck above a Quechan staggered over the railing and crashed to the deck. When they turned the Indian over he was quite dead.

Chan Loo appeared then, a rifle in his hand, a wide-eyed blanched look on his face.

Patronoff narrowed an eye at the Chinese man. "You done this, Chan?"

"He going upee to cabin. He going to stealee gold! I shootee."

Patronoff was clearly unhappy about this. He glanced around at the Indians aboard who were suddenly strung tight as a spring trap.

"Damn," Patronoff said.

"He going to stealee gold!" Chan said again.

"Well, what's done is done." Patronoff looked at the nearest Quechan. "I warned you to stay off my boat. Look what it done to you. Get your friend out of here."

The Indians picked up the dead man and carried him forward in a hurry. Patronoff had the gangplank lowered in place and lent a hand.

Mandell made his way forward with the others and noted the grim uneasiness among the crew and passengers. Then he was aware of the curious way Rose was studying him. Suddenly the amount of explaining he had to do seemed a formidable mountain's worth.

23

The Quechans loaded the dead man onto his horse and helped Olley up onto his. The chief's son was still dazed. They mounted up and rode back into the bluffs above the river. Harrison Mandell leaned against a tarp-covered pile of mining machinery on the deck of the *Bad Water* watching them move off, and a more dejected lot he couldn't remember seeing. A voice at his back startled him.

"I thought it odd when you seemed confused over the Apex Law."

Mandell wheeled around. Rose Haven was standing there, and her pinched glare set him back on his heels.

"And the way you cleverly sidestepped any questions having to do with mining. At first I thought it only modesty. But now I see that I was wrong. Wrong about a lot of things."

Mandell immediately assumed his innocent routine. It was one he was normally good at. Just now, however, his heart wasn't in it. His heart, he was discovering to his dismay, had a mind of its own. The words that came next did not ring with even a trace of truth — and he knew it.

"Whatever are you talking about, Rose?"

"*Miss* Haven, if you please." She eyed his pocket. "Since when do mining engineers need brass knuckles? Or lock picks, like a common burglar? And all that nonsense about graduating from the Colorado School of Mines! It flowed smooth as cream, as if you had rehearsed it just for me. Lies! All lies! Oh, I was so foolish to have believed it. What are you, Mr. Mandell? A common thief? Are you here to swindle the rest of us? It is so perfectly clear now. You drop innuendo and accusations so that I begin to distrust everyone on board. Slowly you draw me in, like a fish on a hook. Why? What unseemly plans did you have in mind for me, Mr. Mandell?"

"Miss Haven, I can assure you —"

"Certainly you can. You are so smooth with words, Mr. Mandell. How easy it is for you to talk your way out of any situation — as if you have been doing it all your life."

"If you will give me a moment to explain —"

"I don't like being lied to. I don't like being used. I feel soiled, and I will thank you not to speak to me for the remainder of the trip." Rose turned her back on him and strode to the staircase. Marshal Dern Turnbough was suddenly at her side, as if he'd been waiting in the dark for this opportunity, but she gave him a quick look that said she wasn't going to put up with any of his foolishness either, and walked on by and up the stairs.

Turnbough studied Mandell, then followed her up the stairs.

Harrison Mandell was suddenly aware of a wide hole that had ripped open his spirit. He had done everything right. Allan Pinkerton would have been proud. But still his cover was nearly destroyed, and worse, Rose despised him now. Just the same, he had to carry through with the job he had agreed to do. Despite all she thought of him, he had to remain Harrison Mandell, Mining Engineer.

Living a life of lies had never been easy. Allan Pinkerton told him once years earlier that working undercover was a little like being unfaithful to a loving wife — especially when relationships form — and they usually did during the course of a job. Only, up to now, Mandell had easily separated the professional side of his life from the private, never allowing the personal end to forge those kinds of attachments.

But something was different here, and it had not been planned for. . . .

Chan Loo's voice cried out like a death wail in the night, and a moment later the Chinese handyman burst from the main cabin doorway running a circle around the boiler deck, pulling hair with both hands, and chattering away in Chinese like a Gatling gun at full crank.

Rose rushed to his side, tried to calm the man, but got only incomprehensible babble and some panicky hand thrusts at the open doorway.

Turnbough stepped past her into the cabin as Mandell mounted the stairs along with McPeevy, the Mexicans, and Captain Patronoff coming back from seeing the Indians on their way.

Even before he reached the main cabin and the table holding the rewards of their hours of excavation, he knew what he would find.

"*Nothing!* It has all been stolen!" McPeevy lamented, on the verge of tears.

"Everyone, calm down!" Patronoff's voice rumbled like thunder through the packed room.

Harrison Mandell stared at the empty spot on the table where all the gold doubloons had been piled earlier. Patronoff's booming command brought the crashing waves of outraged voices to a halt. As the room took on some semblance of order, Mandell went down on his knees to examine the floor beneath the table. He dragged a hand across the dusty wooden planks, rubbed his fingers together, and frowned.

When he stood, every eye was on him. He grinned, brushed at the knees of his trousers, and said, "Dirty down there."

In a moment the agitated voices started up

again. Patronoff barked for silence.

"What will we do now? It is gone, all gone!" This was Loo Han Ling, with eyes welling up. A fat tear traced the slight curve of her cheek. Chan Loo put an arm around his wife's shoulder, himself hard put to control the emotions rising within him.

"We must find the money," McPeevy cried.

"No one will leave the boat until it is found!" Edwardo warned.

Patronoff gave the Mexican an impatient scowl then said, "Well, one thing's for sure, it could not have gotten far."

Turnbough spoke up. "You can't be sure of that. For a while this boat was overrun by them Injuns. Any one of them could have taken the gold and left while we was busy throwing that kid overboard."

"That's right," Darlinda added, "they knew all about the gold. After all, didn't they watch us dig it up?"

"That settles it," Molly said. "I'm all for running down them savages and gettin' back our money!"

At once they agreed to pursue the chief and his band. The Mexicans were the first out the door.

Mandell said, "It wasn't the Indians."

Edwardo halted and came about. "You cannot know that for certain, and while we stand here talking, they ride farther away."

"I do know it for certain," Mandell said.

"Whoever took the gold is still in this room."

Rose Haven said, "Maybe we should first look more closely at ourselves." Her view settled on Mandell. "At least one of us sneaked off while Captain Patronoff and the chief were arguing. And he was gone a good long time before the fight with the chief's son."

Hostile stares burned instantly in his direction.

"That is true." Betty spoke so quietly that their attention was riveted by the stark contrast. "I too saw him leave. Saw him go down toward the captain's cabin."

"You know why I did that," Mandell said, irritated that he would have to come to his own defense.

"No, we don't," Turnbough shot back. The marshal appeared to be taking some delight in Mandell's predicament. "All we know is you ran into the chief's kid. That might have been by accident."

There was general agreement on that point.

"Let's go through his luggage and see if the money's hid there," Molly demanded.

Mandell backed up against the table as the contentious mob pressed forward. He cast about for a way to extradite himself if the situation got out of hand, but all routes of escape were covered. There would be no practical way to resist so many determined adversaries.

"Hold up there!" Patronoff's words rumbled through their midst. "I still ain't convinced the Indians didn't take it."

A scattering of voices added their support to that notion.

Patronoff looked at Mandell. "How can you know for certain that the Indians didn't take it unless you was here to witness it?"

Mandell stepped away from the table, casually closing the distance between himself and the door, and as he did so he said, "When Olley climbed aboard, he was wet. And any other Quechan who managed to come on board would be wet too since the gangplank had been drawn up. Just a moment ago I checked the floor. Not a damp footprint in sight. Look yourself. Not even stray drips such as might fall from their breechclouts or hair." He stopped and took them all in with a sweeping glance. "And if it had been I who took the money, why would I be telling you this? Why would I have spoken up at all when you wanted to take out after the chief?"

Mandell figured it made sense, and he drew in a relieved breath when after a moment of silence the angry faces that had been glaring at him slowly rotated and focused their suspicions onto nearby neighbors.

"Well, what do we do now?" This was Alf Danderfault, standing tall at the rear of the crowd, confounded, his sandy hair disarrayed like an old mop, his eyes concerned.

"It's got to be on the boat!" someone said.

A dozen people went off in a dozen different directions until Patronoff reined them back in. "If we are gonna go through *my* boat, we are gonna do it in an orderly fashion. Alf, Chan, get the lamps lighted so we can see what we're doing. We'll start back at the wheel and work our way forward."

In ten minutes Patronoff had the search party organized. For the next hour Mandell watched from the railing of the hurricane deck as they systematically moved forward, peeking into every conceivable nook and cranny. Patronoff sent a second party down into the cargo hold, and that took a much longer time to go through. By midnight they had all regrouped in the main cabin and fell about exhausted, nodding off to sleep.

Throughout the evening, Rose Haven had pointedly ignored Mandell, and now she joined the other women behind the curtain while several men met at the bar where the liquor had begun to run too freely.

Mandell poured himself a whiskey. The conversation moving through the scattered knots of men seemed to be heading in a most unhealthy direction. The loss of the gold and the lateness of the hour had worn their patience thin. There were vague accusations handed about — no one was spared — but the brunt of the suspicions were falling on the Mexicans.

205

Tommy Morgan seemed to have gotten drunk the quickest, and he finally wheeled away from the bar, pushed his spectacles up the bridge of his nose, and said overly loud, "I'll wager *they* know exactly where the gold is."

Felix looked over, said something in Spanish to his friends, and stepped toward Morgan. Ramon caught him by the arm, spoke softly. Felix nodded his head, halting his advance.

Morgan was feeling his whiskey. "Those three are no more cooks than I'm President Chester A. Arthur. I'll tell you what they are. Them's bandits. Run up over the border by their own gov'ment, I'll wager. And mark my words, they figured out a way to take the gold whilst we was occupied with the chief. There's three of them, three son of a bitch greasers, and they worked it out among them. I say we teach 'em what for. Beat it out of 'em then ship 'em back down to Mexico where they belong."

Mandell said to Tommy, "Some opinions are best kept to yourself, Morgan."

The pilot turned, unsteady. He'd been hitting the whiskey hard since they had returned from their unsuccessful search of the boat. The next instant his fist shot out. Mandell easily sidestepped it, caught the arm, and twisted it up behind Morgan's back.

"You're drunk," he said. "Go sleep it off

before it gets you hurt, or worse." Mandell shoved the pilot toward the door. Immediately Morgan wheeled, his knuckles bunched. Mandell knocked aside the fist and shot a short jab to the man's chin that staggered the pilot out the door and back against the deck railing.

The passengers swarmed out onto the deck after them.

Morgan came back with a wide swing, but he was not a fighter, and at the moment he was too drunk to care. Mandell set him back on his heels, doubled him over, and straightened him up like a barrel stave with an uppercut. Morgan tottered then collapsed.

He heard disgruntled complaints at his back. When he turned no one made a move. Turnbough stood in the doorway, leaning his lanky frame against the jamb, but Morgan was nothing to him and after a moment he stepped back inside to the whiskey.

The Mexicans went down the dark gallery by themselves. Mandell glanced back at the crew standing about, then down at Morgan. The man would wake up bruised and aching, but at least he would wake up. The detective knew the Mexicans would not have long endured Morgan's angry words, and they would have shut his mouth in a more permanent fashion.

"Someone give me a hand with him?"

A grumble moved through the crew. Alf

Danderfault stepped forward, hefted the smaller man over his arm, and said, "I'll put him to bed." He carried Morgan down the stairs to the main deck where the crew would bed down this night. No one wanted to spend it ashore considering what had happened with the Indians.

The crowd broke up, some back to the liquor, others searching out a place to sleep. The general depression had infected the boat like a plague. Mandell felt its sting doubly as he stepped to the railing and stared out at the dark bluffs. The money didn't matter all that much to him, and he had little problem putting it temporarily out of mind. What proved to be a much greater problem was trying not to think of Rose, or how he could have handled it differently. But there had been no other way, he knew. He worked for Allan Pinkerton, and that was where his loyalties lay — or so he tried to convince himself.

Far away on top of the bluffs he caught a glimpse of a campfire. The Quechans, no doubt. Now with one of their own dead, he couldn't help but wonder how long it would take before the old chief decided to even up the score.

24

In the darkness, Mandell heard Darlinda's soft, unrestrained laughter, and Dern Turnbough's voice, low and suggestive. The sounds of their footsteps diminished, and when Mandell glanced back where the paddle wheel was hidden in shadows, he could no longer see the two of them, but fragments of spoken words and muffled giggles made their way forward.

McPeevy stepped out of the main cabin and glanced along the dark gallery. He spied Mandell standing at the railing and came over.

"You're up late," Mandell said.

"Aye. I might say the same about ye." He glanced aft. "And there be others too keepin' late hours."

Mandell nodded at the flicker of light from the faroff campfire. "I am wondering what to expect from them next."

"Aye. It was a bad business for the Chinaman to be shooting the Indian like that. And still the gold was made off with. Bad business. Saints, it bodes not well, methinks." McPeevy inclined his head at the door to the darkened main cabin. "I could not sleep thinking over the day. Heard voices out on the deck and figured I wasn't the only one. If I have got to think, I do a better job of it on my two feet than on my back."

"The King asleep?"

McPeevy laughed. "You know how kings be. They care not a twit about gold and such; what they need, they take. By taxes or thievery, they are both the same thing. He's sleeping like a babe."

Mandell turned back to the dark landscape and considered his next question carefully. "You know her, don't you?"

It caught McPeevy off guard. "Whatever you talking about, man?"

Mandell hid a grin into the darkness. McPeevy's tone had answered his question. "The redhead — Darlinda. You know her from somewhere."

"I should say not," McPeevy denied instantly, but he cut that line short and did not speak for a moment. When he did his words were heavy, as if burdened by a dark secret he had kept bottled up, waiting only for a friendly ear to tell it to.

"Aye, I know the woman — or I should say, I have made her acquaintance a couple of times. Many years ago. In Kansas City. I du'na think she remembers me. Frankly, I di'na expect to run into her ever again. I thought for certain the lass was still in jail, or the gallows had stretched her pretty neck."

"You knew her . . . professionally?"

McPeevy averted his face. "I was a client, I am ashamed to admit. Played my pipes a time or two for the lass, in my room above the Kansas City Harvey House, and she seemed to enjoy it. Showed her appreciation in a most energetic manner." He looked at Mandell, suddenly intent. "I did not know she was a married woman at the time. How could I? It's not the sort of thing you ask of a working girl."

"She is a married prostitute?" Mandell lifted an eyebrow in a bit of humor.

"She *was* a married prostitute. Saints, the story was all over the Kansas City newspapers. Reckon she must have had a row with her husband one night because sure enough she killed the man. Beat in his brains with an iron skillet, she did. Well, they arrested her to be sure, and I di'na hear a thing further of the incident. I was most taken aback when I saw her the other day on the street in Yuma, for the first time in" — he thought — "in over five years, I calculate. I suppose she managed to escape the law somehow and make it into the territories. It's where many criminals find safety. The last I read in the papers, she was to be tried for murder."

"Maybe she was tried and acquitted."

"No, I du'na think so. I would have heard that. No, she must have escaped. I have tried to keep out of the lass's way, hoping she would not remember me. I du'na think she does."

"She seems fetchin' with the marshal."

"Aye. It's her job," he said understandingly.

The next morning the general air of dejection aboard the boat gave way to more immediate necessities, and the *Bad Water*'s paddle wheel was soon repaired and pummeling the river's current behind a full head of steam. Marshal Turnbough woke late complaining of stomach pains and dizziness. He looked pallid. Captain Patronoff went to his cabin where the medical supplies were kept and fetched the marshal some asafetida and whiskey mixed with water. The marshal cursed bad tequila. Mandell mused over worms at the bottom of the bottles, and if that had anything to do with Turnbough's sudden illness. Darlinda seemed happy enough — perhaps she had not drunk any tequila the night before.

Rose remained coolly aloof.

McPeevy had lost the King sometime during the night and was running around the boat calling for the big tomcat.

"Saints! He has never run off like this before," McPeevy told Mandell some time later, mopping the sweat from his face and neck with a dingy handkerchief. The Scotsman cast a glance at the desolate landscape passing beyond the railing. "Ye du'na suppose he somehow got ashore last night?"

Anything was likely, but there was no reason to worry McPeevy more than he was already. "He probably caught a juicy rat and is somewhere right now sleeping it off." Mandell gave a short laugh, recalling the cat's predilection toward alcohol. "Or maybe he got into some of Turnbough's bad tequila."

McPeevy narrowed his view up at the main cabin. "Saints, what if the marshal has harmed King Robert! You figure he's up to it?"

Mandell frowned. "I wouldn't put it past the man. He does have a powerful hatred of felines, but before you think the worse, give the boat another look. Have you tried the cargo hold?"

"Nae. It's not a place for the likes of me to go a crawling about. Perhaps one of the crew —"

"Tell you what, Gilligan," Mandell said, seeing an opportunity in this that would not draw suspicion. "I'll crawl down there and have a look myself for you. The old King knows me. He might decide to lay low if one of the crew goes looking."

"Aye! Would ye do that?"

"Just give me a few minutes. Something I need to see to first."

McPeevy seemed instantly encouraged. "It's

the sort of mischief King Robert might do, after all, isn't it?" he said as if to reassure himself.

"Disappearing is one of those things cats are good at," Mandell agreed.

Mandell knocked at the open door. "Can I come in?"

Tommy Morgan looked over his shoulder. His hands gripped the big helm, and there was tenseness about the man that grew more obvious when he discovered who it was who had knocked. "Why not? You ain't never asked permission before," Morgan said, turning back to the treacherous water ahead.

"Captain not around?"

"You can find him down in the engine room."

"Actually, it is you I want to talk to, Tommy."

Morgan glanced over, surprised, then back to the more weighty business of piloting the *Bad Water* around the snags and roiling water.

Mandell spied the black book of bound charts on a ledge beneath a window. He stepped near it and gazed out at the painful glare off the water ahead.

"What about?" Morgan said, surly, but with a note of curiosity as well.

"I wanted to say I was sorry about last night. It was nothing personal."

Morgan didn't speak at once. Eyes ahead, view firmly fixed upon the water, but it was plain this was not what he had expected. After a moment he said, "From what Alf tells me, I guess I deserved it. He says I was getting some out of hand." Morgan's voice had lost its edge.

Mandell inclined an eye at the open book. The river — the section they were traveling at this moment, he gathered — was sketched out in black ink, with red and blue hash marks depicting shoals or shallow water. Numbers that might have indicated depth had been carefully penned along the way. There were perhaps twenty pages of charts already turned over, and maybe that many left on the other side of the book: the river still remaining to be covered.

"I was watching the Mexicans. You were very nearly about to lose more than a fistfight. One of them was looking for blood, any blood, after that gold disappeared. The day had been bad enough. I didn't figure we needed another killing as well."

"Whiskey tends to oil my tongue. I know that, pretty much stay away from the stuff. But I was — well, I guess we all were — so disappointed. For a little while there I thought about buying my own boat. Most pilots have that dream, you know." His brow wrinkled and he pushed the spectacles up the sweat-slick bridge of his nose. He looked at

Mandell. "Come to think, you were about the only one who wasn't disappointed."

There was confusion suddenly in Morgan's face that Mandell sensed was about to turn into suspicion.

He grinned. "That's because I know the gold is still on this boat."

"Where?"

"Don't know that . . . yet."

"How can you be so certain?"

"The Indians didn't take it, although the foxy old chief had his eye on it, and he stuck with a pretty flimsy diversion to allow his men time to swim up to the *Bad Water* and climb aboard. But we know they didn't take it. Chan made certain of that, and I checked the floor around the table. They never got near to it. So that means whoever took it is still on board, and so is the gold."

"What if they tossed it overboard figgerin' on coming back for it? It ain't on board. Been over this boat from bow to stern."

"No one did that. The gold is still on board. We just haven't found where it is hidden. We passengers wouldn't have thrown it overboard. No way any one of us would know where to look for it again. And the crew wouldn't have either, considering how quickly this river changes its banks. A new shoal where a day before there was open water? They know this river too well to chance that much gold to her capricious ways."

Morgan frowned. "The Mexicans?"

"I don't think so. They're up to something, but it's not stealing gold."

"You got it all figured out, Mandell, don't you?"

"Not all of it." It was time to change the direction of the conversation. "Any sign of the Indians?"

"No. They crawled off somewhere to lick their wounds. But they'll be back. They love a good show," Morgan said bitterly, "and there ain't nothin' more entertaining in this wilderness than watching a steamboat run up on a shoal."

"You pretty much know where the shoals and snags are, though."

"I know the big ones. And the ones what was here two weeks ago. It's the new slides that hang us up." He lifted his chin to the high ridge of bluffs, at this point removed from the water's edge a quarter mile. "Up there you can spot them shoals miles off. Down here on the water it is hard to tell. Whenever there's a new one, I make note of it in that book."

Mandell glanced at the volume by his elbow. "This book?"

"That's right."

He picked it up and looked at it as if seeing it for the first time. "You got the whole river in here?"

"Not the *whole* river. Just enough to get us

up to the Bad Water Mine, and then some. Not all that much navigable water beyond the mine. At least, not for a vessel the size of *Bad Water*."

"What is up above the mine?"

"Nothing worth mentioning. A couple small settlements. Some prospectors scraping at the rock in the hopes of striking color. There's a cavalry fort, Fort Whipple, near Prescott, up beyond the Bill Williams River — after it turns into the Santa Maria. They sometimes comes down the Colorado to Yuma, especially when they got prisoners to take to the new penitentiary. The army's got a small steamboat what makes it back a ways to a landing. The Bill Bill runs into the Colorado a little north of here. We'll be makin' its mouth tomorrow morning sometime. The Bad Water Mine ain't but another half day beyond."

"Mmmm."

"You find that interesting?"

"Huh? Oh, no. I was just thinking it was about time Loo Han Ling was getting something together for lunch." Mandell thumbed a few pages in the book and said, "I'll be happy to see this trip end."

"I'm most happy to see 'em all end. Every one."

"What is this?"

Morgan glanced at the page Mandell had open, and the place where his finger had settled.

"That's called Diablo Bend — officially. Every one just calls it the Narrows."

"Shore comes in pretty close."

Morgan gave that an indifferent shrug. "Yeah, but it's no problem. Water is swift there. Cuts a clean, deep channel. Most of two fathoms deep."

Mandell turned the book back to its original page and set it back on the shelf. "That is reassuring to hear. Well, I'm going to see if there is anything ready for lunch. Later, Tommy."

Mandell left the wheelhouse and skipped down the stairs. He tried not to let the smile show too much.

25

Darlinda called to him as he came off the upper staircase. She had been standing in the doorway of the main cabin, squeezing her hands, concern in her eyes. "Have you seen Dern, Mr. Mandell?" she asked him.

He drew up, hand upon the banister of the wide steps descending to the main deck, and looked back, struck again by the brilliance of her red hair. "Last I saw of him, he was still on his cot, looking seasick."

"But he had begun to feel better. We went for a walk. Stopped down at the engine room because Dern wanted to talk to the captain. I left him there for a few minutes and when I returned, Dern had disappeared. The captain says he doesn't know where. I've searched all over and can't find him. It's not that big a boat that a man can lose himself. I thought perhaps you had seen him?"

Mandell realized he was staring again. This attractive, if somewhat overly painted — not unlike some Indians he had known, he mused — woman hardly looked the type who could have beaten out the brains of her husband with an iron skillet. But then, he had learned early on in his career as a Pinkerton Detective that appearances meant nothing when tracking down a criminal. He recalled Molly's stern look when Darlinda had described what she would like to do to Olley, and now he understood why. Molly knew this woman's past, and probably Betty did too.

He smiled, easing the scrutinizing glare from his face. "I'm sure the marshal will turn up. As you say, it isn't so large a boat that a man can easily lose himself for very long. If I see him, I will tell him you are looking."

"Thank you." She removed herself from noon sunlight, but the cabin wouldn't be any cooler, and neither would be the *Bad Water*'s cargo hold.

"After another one of Captain Patronoff's beers?" Rose's voice was both reproachful and laden with caustic humor.

Mandell had taken care that he was alone before lifting the bow hatch. No one had been around — or so he had thought. So, she was keeping an eye on him, and being discreet about it. How much did she suspect — how much did she know?

"Mighty hot to be out in the sun when there is no need for it, Rose," he said, and grinned innocently.

Her face was sunburned, and flushed, and despite her best effort to stand erect — Miss Filvia would be proud — the merciless sun beat her down. Her hair, pinned up as best she could manage, dangled long, limp strands to her shoulders. It, like the rest of her, needed a good scrubbing. She was wearing the same velvet-trimmed traveling dress she had worn the day before. It too had long ago wilted from the heat. Her hat was the only article of clothing that appeared to have endured the trip unscathed. "The heat doesn't seem to be stopping you," she said.

"I thought you didn't want to speak to me the rest of the trip."

"I do not. You are a liar, and a thief. And I still think you had something to do with the gold disappearing last night."

"And by following me around you intend to discover where I hid it?"

"Perhaps. Or maybe I'll discover who you really are."

"Perhaps you will only discover that I am exactly who I say I am."

She laughed. "I doubt that. Look at what you're up to now. Sneaking around the cargo hold again where you have no legitimate business being."

"You know that for sure?"

Despite the misery of the heat, she managed to flash a superior smile. "Yes, I am sure of it, although I am also certain you will come up with a very believable argument to prove me incorrect."

"Mr. Mandell is looking for my cat."

Rose came about. "Oh! Mr. McPeevy!"

"King Robert the Second is missing," he said, his distress plain. "Mr. Mandell was kind enough to offer to crawl down in that awful place and look for him."

"He was?"

"Aye. And I wish ye would not keep him from it now, miss."

Mandell said, "You are welcome to accompany me if you wish to keep an eye on me," knowing full well she would refuse. McPeevy could not have picked a better moment to show up.

"No, thank you." Rose turned severely on her heels and strode away.

McPeevy patted his head with the crumpled cloth. "I do hope ye find him. Otherwise, he can'na be nowhere else except —"

McPeevy's eyes flicked briefly at the reddish water roiling past them.

"— well, I du'na want to think about that. Good luck, Harry."

No animal with any sense about him would have chosen to remain in the oven of the *Bad Water*'s cargo hold any longer than necessary. Mandell knew this almost the instant he crouched below the low deck where the trapped heat was like a wet wool blanket pulled suddenly over him. Just the same — and for the benefit of the man standing only a few feet overhead — he called out King

Robert's name as he crawled back toward the hidden icebox.

Once below the cabins, however, he ceased imploring the King to show himself and moved silently through the gloom, then pulled up alongside the padlocked latch. In a moment he had it unlocked. The rush of cooler air as he hauled the heavy door open did little to temper the heat of the cargo hold. He struck a match. Everything inside the icebox was exactly as it had been the day before. His eyebrows drew together. He had been so certain he would find the gold hidden there. This had been the only place left unsearched!

Moving the match side to side shifted the shadows about some inside the box, but the bottled beer and the untapped keg were the only items there. He struggled to move the heavy keg aside, and behind it found only more coiled copper tubing. No gold. The rush of river water coursing through them sang out into the sweltering hold, merging with the pounding heartbeat of the engines nearby.

He studied the interior of the box, but could discover no clues. After removing a bottle of Patronoff's beer for his own use, he closed, locked, and leaned back against the door to rethink all the pieces of the puzzle.

"Did you find him?" Patronoff asked when Mandell climbed up out of the bow hatch.

There was an intentness in the big captain's dark eyes that burned like embers. His beard glistened as if a coal pile sprinkled with morning dew, and the cigar, shoved immediately back between the teeth, shifted from the left corner of his lips to the right.

Mandell found himself wondering what all the urgency was over a missing cat. There about him stood three deckhands, Molly and Betty, and Chan Loo — all looking concerned. Darlinda was a little way off and, to his left, was McPeevy with the empty valise in hand, looking forlorn.

"I didn't find him," Mandell said.

"Oh, my," Molly whispered, and shook her head. "He must have gone overboard."

Mandell grinned. "Before we think the worst, let's look around for him a bit longer. Like I told Gilligan, maybe he caught himself a big, savory rat and is off somewhere digesting it."

Their faces turned toward him, a mix of surprise and disgust.

"That is not at all funny," Darlinda said. "He didn't like you all that much, and he had his reasons, and you didn't like him either, I know, but that's no reason to say such an awful thing!"

Mandell realized then that it wasn't a cat that they were talking about at all.

"Turnbough is still missing?"

The expression on their faces was answer enough.

26

Patronoff ordered the boat put into shore.

"No one is to leave," the captain said, and then he took Alf and Chan with him back toward the stern to begin another search. This time for Turnbough. Two decks up, Tommy Morgan had stepped out of the wheelhouse and casually leaned against the shore-side railing, a rifle cradled in the crook of one arm. Whether it was there to guard against Indians, or to make certain the captain's orders were obeyed, Mandell didn't know.

Edwardo eyed the pilot too, and Mandell heard his softly spoken words to his friends, as he cast a glance at the shore. The detective tried to read the meaning in that, but the possibilities were endless. The Mexicans went off to poke some more around the piles of deck cargo and peek under tarps. They were determined, it seemed, to find the missing gold single-handed.

Molly gathered up her resolve, despite the oppressive heat, and said to Darlinda and Betty, "Come on, girls. Might as well lend a hand. It beats sitting around and waiting."

"I find it strange," McPeevy said thoughtfully, "that King Robert and the marshal are both gone."

"Another coincidence?"

McPeevy looked at the detective. "Aye, and I recall that ye du'na believe in coincidences."

"Just say that I get skeptical when too many start coming my way."

"Aye. And myself as well."

"Come on."

"Where be we off to?"

"To look for your cat. And maybe find the marshal as well."

Rose intercepted Mandell and McPeevy halfway down the gallery and immediately levered herself up onto her toes to smell his breath.

"I knew it!" she said, as if the odor of beer somehow vindicated her earlier suspicions. "You could not let the opportunity slip through your sticky fingers, could you?"

At that moment Patronoff, Alf, and Chan came around the back side of the boat. They had made their way across the stilled paddle wheel, using its paddles as a bridge. They began working their way forward, opening doors as they came. The captain looked worried. Losing passengers was not the sort of thing a riverboat captain liked to have show up on his record — even if the record was already a slight bit tarnished.

"Perhaps Captain Patronoff ought to know

227

about your skill with lock picks?" Rose said.

McPeevy looked from Rose to the detective, somewhat confused.

Mandell replied quietly, "If you could give me a few moments to explain —"

There was the sound of a door handle being rattled, and then Chan's voice. "No can open upee."

"That door shouldn't be locked." Patronoff gave it a try. They were standing in front of the storage room where the crew kept their belongings. Patronoff said, "I've a key in my cabin," and went forward two doors to his own cabin.

Rose glanced back at Mandell. "Explain? I see no reason why I should allow you the opportunity to lie to me again." Her brown eyes narrowed.

He lowered his voice further. "Have you ever considered that there may be a good reason for my discretion?"

She looked at him, eyes at once huge with amazement. "I can think of no good reason to —"

Patronoff burst from his cabin. "The key is missing," he snapped. "Where in the devil . . . ? Well, come on, let's go see if one of the hands has it."

McPeevy mopped his forehead. "I du'na think I'm up to carry on with this in this blasted heat. A bit of shade perhaps, and something cool to drink."

"Why don't we all find something cool to drink?" Mandell said, and then added pointedly at Rose when he read the look that had come to her face, "*Up*stairs."

"Are you feeling ill?" Rose asked McPeevy.

"Nae. It is only the heat."

"Or maybe what Turnbough has is catching," she said.

"I hope it is not."

Up in the main cabin Loo Han Ling served them tepid tea. McPeevy seemed to revitalize once out of the direct heat of the sun. Rose sat across the table from Mandell, sipping her drink, eyeing him curiously over the top of her glass.

"All right," she said finally. "If you care to explain your suspicious actions, I am willing to listen. But I'm not easily convinced."

Molly and her girls had given up the search for Turnbough too, and were lounging about the cabin like three colorful, wilted cucumber leaves. Molly's attention pricked up at this.

Mandell made a wry smile. There were too many ears about at the moment. He said to Rose, "Later."

"I knew it. You are so very clever, but when your bluff is called, you back down."

At the doorway, Felix stepped inside. The Mexican looked the place over, as if trying to discover one inch of rafter space or one square foot of floor that he had not already scoured. He opened the lower cupboard doors on the liquor cabinet for perhaps the tenth time, frowned, closed them, and turned slowly about, studying the room.

At the back where the women slept, he nudged aside baggage with the toe of his boot, then, with concern clearly marked upon his face, left the cabin.

"They are a determined lot, they are," McPeevy said.

"At least we know *they* didn't take the gold," Rose said, slanting an eye at Mandell.

He winced under her stare. "The question now is not *who* took the gold, but who took *Turnbough*."

"And King Robert," McPeevy put in.

"And if you find both of them, you will find the gold too?" she inquired.

All Mandell could offer on that notion was a shrug of his shoulders. That was one of the pieces of the puzzle he hadn't yet fitted in place.

Edwardo was keeping an eye on the main cabin doorway. He and Ramon stood in the shadow of the boat's upper stories, and when Felix appeared at the main cabin door, Edwardo waved an arm at him to come down.

Felix started down the stairs.

Ramon said to Edwardo, "He puts too much effort into finding that treasure."

Edwardo grinned. His dark cheeks were smudged with the coarse stubble of a new beard, now beginning to fill in the skin around his black mustache. "The gold would have been a nice prize to take away with us, no?"

"The gold would be a fine prize indeed, and I too would like to carry it back to Mexico. But that is not the reason for us being here. I wonder if Felix has forgotten that reason."

Edwardo dismissed that notion with a wave of his hand. "He has not forgotten. Like all of us who have come north, he knows the importance of the revolution. Diaz must not be reelected as president, and Felix knows the hearts of the people are with Carlos. Felix understands that if we fail to take Carlos from the hands of the Yankee soldiers, the revolution will fail. He knows that as well as you and I. The only difference is, my friend, to us Carlos may be an honored leader of the revolution, but he is not our flesh and blood. He is neither my brother nor Felix's brother. You, my friend, are too close to the problem. Perhaps it would have been better if you had remained in Mexico."

"Never! My place is here with the men who will rescue my brother from the army prison."

Felix came around a mound of cargo. "Your words carry, Ramon."

Ramon glanced at him. "It makes little difference. The English-speaking people have no time to learn our language. We must learn theirs, but they are too arrogant to waste their efforts on ours."

Felix's easy grin seemed to quench Ramon's sudden fire. "This is true, but they do not have to understand the words to understand the emotion behind them."

Edwardo said, "Save your fighting for the Yankee soldiers, Ramon." He glanced around the heavily laden boat and went on, "If that pilot can keep from running aground until the morning, we may yet succeed in our goal. Then we will have enough fighting to keep us all happy, no?"

Ramon grunted. "I hope Diego has had no trouble getting our men into position, and that they will be waiting when we stop that army boat. I would hate to be sitting on the bottom of this river with no place to go but down to the Yuma prison."

"At least you will have your brother for company," Edwardo said, and laughed. But Ramon remained unsmiling.

Felix said, "In the meantime, I will continue to search for the gold. It would be a shame to let it sink to the bottom too."

Edwardo said, "Tomorrow morning, early. That is when I have determined we will be in the Narrows. We must be ready to move swiftly then. Do not let tequila fog your brain tonight."

★ ★ ★

Up in the main cabin, Harrison Mandell let the curtain fall back in place and turned away from the window. Acute observation — studying a fly's wing beneath the lens of a microscope, as Rose had put it — often told more about a person than their own carefully edited words. It was one of those skills Mandell had honed through the years. Some people read books. He read people: the way they gestured, the way they stood, the intenseness of their expressions. It was the small things that revealed what they thought, what they held important, the plans they made.

He returned to the table.

"What's that scowl for?" Rose asked, giving him a penetrating stare.

"What scowl, Rose?"

She threw up her hands. "You're an absolutely infuriating man!"

Mandell raised his eyebrows at this outburst. Pure innocence. Wounded. He smiled at her just the same.

Rose lurched from the table, shaking with anger, and strode out the door.

McPeevy glanced up, only remotely distracted by her outburst, and in another moment his eyes returned to the empty valise at his feet.

Mandell wandered back to the window after a few minutes, but the Mexicans were no longer on the main deck where he could see them.

27

Rose Haven had been only half correct.

They found Marshal Dern Turnbough and King Robert the Second . . . together . . . but they did not find the gold.

Captain Patronoff had questioned every hand aboard the *Bad Water*. None had seen the key to the storage room. In the end, Patronoff ordered the door smashed open.

In the sweltering air, the odor that burst from the room drove them back. And the next instant King Robert bounded out onto the deck and halted, as if ready to fight the world.

"King Robert!" McPeevy exclaimed, having come out of the main cabin above them and to the railing to determine why a husky riverman had been driving his shoulder into the door below.

The cat meowed, its fur erect as if under the mystic influence of an electric current, making the animal look twice its size. McPeevy and Mandell came down the stairs and around the side gallery.

King Robert was not sure he wanted to be confined again, even if it was McPeevy himself attempting to pick him up, but it was only a moment of indecision before the fat tomcat was in the Scotsman's arms, purring like a top.

"Aye, my darlin'. Ye got yourself locked up, ye did." McPeevy sniffed the air and screwed up his face.

Mandell stepped around him and looked into the storage room where Patronoff and Chan Loo were hanging back a discreet distance.

The smell that emerged struck a hammer's blow and drove him back. The heat had energized it into a foul barrier that very nearly kept them all at bay as efficiently as if there had been a grizzly bear in there with Turnbough.

Diarrhea and vomit.

Hours old. Dried in places. Soupy in others. Mandell turned away in disgust then gathered his resolve to do what he knew he had to.

Molly, Darlinda, and Betty had stopped a little ways back, craning their necks. Rose Haven inched along a wall but kept well back.

Patronoff turned to them. "You ladies don't want to see this."

Darlinda came forward, as if drawn along by an unseen hand, and cried suddenly, "Dern!"

Her eyes expanded, then she covered her mouth and turned away.

It didn't take long for the news to get around the little boat, and in two minutes everyone on board had gathered there, lingering back a healthy distance where the odor was bearable.

Mandell held a breath and stepped inside the storage room. Dern Turnbough was sitting up against the wall. His head was canted to one side, his eyes were bulging. A spasm had clamped his teeth down tight like a vise, yellowed lips peeled back. The marshal's tongue dangled from the few threads of tissue that had managed to remain intact.

Slanting sunlight showed the yellow of his skin. The small amount of dried blood on his vest from the severed tongue was black and hard.

Mandell retreated from the room, spun toward the river to draw in a breath. When he turned back he saw the glint of black flint in Patronoff's eye where the captain stood thinking.

Aside, Darlinda was weeping into a dirty handkerchief, and saying something about that cat, and asthma, and wasn't it just an awful thing to have happen.

"Chan, Alf. Better hale him out of there," Patronoff said.

Alf Danderfault frowned, his nose wrinkling some, and he said, "What will we do with him once we do, Captain?"

"We'll bury him," Patronoff said. "It's the Christian thing to do."

"No, no. Just throwee into river." Chan pinched his nose and made a face.

"We'll give him a decent burial. No argument about it."

Alf and Chan pulled the dead man from the small room and laid him out on the deck. Patronoff glared down at Turnbough a second then strode up to the wheelhouse and in a minute came back to disperse the crowd.

"How long a delay, *Señor* Captain?" Edwardo asked when the captain moved past him.

"As long as it takes to dig a hole, mister," Patronoff said, not pausing his determined strides, as if he had up a head of steam to do the task, and he wanted to see it through with no delays.

Mandell heard the bell clang, and the engines change their rhythm, felt a lurch as the boat angled for the Arizona side of the river. He was aware of the captain above him, and then Patronoff's rumbling voice. "What is it you are looking for, Mandell?"

The detective set Turnbough's arm back onto the deck and stood. "I'm trying to determine what killed the marshal."

Rose had remained a little ways away, watching, and now the detective noted the odd look in her brown eyes, as if her brain was attempting to digest conflicting information. Well, it was what Mandell did all the time — it was what he was good at.

Patronoff huffed. "It's plain how he died. We all knowed how Turnbough got sick around cats. Somehow he was snooping around where he didn't belong and got himself locked up accidental. He probably didn't even realize that McPeevy's cat was in the storage room, and by the time he found out, it was too late. He couldn't breathe enough to cry out, and it don't take but a few minutes like that in this heat, to pass out. Afterward it was only a matter of time before he died.

"The diarrhea?"

"Hell, everyone knows a man shits his pants once he dies."

"The vomit?"

Patronoff shrugged his shoulders. "He was sick. Had been all morning. Who knows what he had? I don't find it a thing to worry about."

Mandell pulled at his chin thoughtfully. He could see there was no sense mentioning Turnbough's color, or the red rash on his arm and wrist, or how the door got locked in the first place. Patronoff had made up his mind on the matter. He said, "Well, Captain, I guess there is nothing more to learn here. You got it pretty much figured out." Then he added, "This gets rid of one of your problems."

Patronoff glared at him. "What's that supposed to mean?"

Mandell smiled disarmingly. "Nothing. Only that I was thinking it might look bad on your record if you had lost Turnbough overboard. This way, the incident is explained away credibly, with no loose ends."

Patronoff studied him warily, as if trying to read something in the detective's expression. But Mandell made certain his easy smile revealed nothing. "That's right," Patronoff said, "and that's how it goes down in my log."

Mandell nodded his head. "Certainly, Captain. I'll lend a hand digging the hole when it's time." He stepped over to Rose Haven then, and she peered up into his face as if in a trance. "You should not be down here to see this," he said.

"I've never seen a dead body before," she answered quietly, awed by the experience. "At least not one that hadn't been prepared first." She looked at him suddenly, sharp and clear again. "What was it you were searching for on his arm?" Her eyes narrowed. "And don't give me another of your patent lies and cover it over with honey to make it easy to swallow. You were looking for something."

He took her by the arm and she did not resist. As he walked her forward, away from the grisly scene on the aft deck, he said, "Like I told Patronoff, I wanted to determine what really killed Turnbough."

"But the captain —"

"The captain is looking for a neat way to explain a messy affair," Mandell said, stopping to look into her eyes and admire the way they widened with curiosity and intelligence. "Turnbough did not die of an acute attack of asthma, that I can assure you."

"If not the asthma, then what? Or should I be asking then *who?*"

He shrugged his shoulders and resumed escorting her forward and up the stairs. "That, I haven't figured out yet, but I'm working on it."

The detective felt deceitful even as he spoke it, but the honey was apparently sweet enough, and Rose swallowed it without question.

The ceremony was simple and brief. The heat and mosquitoes helped expedite the affair, and the nervous impatience of the three Mexicans was a sharp prod that brought on a swift "Amen" and the shutting of the Book. Spades bit the dry, sandy soil and the cool darkness of the earth gave Turnbough his final embrace.

The Indians showed up for the funeral too, keeping their distance, yet it was enough to remind the passengers and crew of the *Bad Water* that they were still near. As Mandell watched them he had a nagging sense that their easy, friendly presence of only a day earlier was somehow changed. They sat straight on the backs of their ponies, alert, their rifles in clear view across their legs or propped on a hip. The time for good-natured bartering was past. If these Quechans could, they were going to take what they wanted, be it woman or gold — or most likely both.

Gangplank drawn up, the engines resumed their rhythmic pulse and the little steamboat resumed bucking the current, which had grown swifter now as the river was slowly being pinched by steep walls of stone ahead.

At the bow, Edwardo grabbed hold of a spar and leaned forward, peering ahead, then up at the flat overhanging ledges of land rising two hundred or more feet above rough water. At the base of the escarpments broken rocks stabbed up through the eddying currents like the back-spikes of a half-submerged dragon.

The Mexican spent considerable time watching the river growing more wild. It was a small display of the true nature of this artery of water where another hundred miles north no steamboat could ever hope to navigate. Finally Edwardo stepped back away from the forward edge, fully absorbed in some thought that drew his black eyebrows together and hitched his tight lips off to one side. He ascended the stairway and went into the main cabin.

From up on the hurricane deck, Mandell

shifted his view back out onto the restless water, then over his shoulder at the wheelhouse where Tommy Morgan was wrestling with the helm, fighting the river to keep the *Bad Water* to the middle of the channel. He'd run this stretch of water before, knew what to expect. Just the same, Mandell suspected the pilot was about to have a new problem to contend with this trip . . . unless he could figure a way to put an end to it.

"It was food poisoning, I tell you!" Molly announced to no one in particular.

Loo Han Ling, who at that very moment was passing around afternoon victuals, took exception to this and pulled the platter of hard-bread sandwiches out from beneath Molly's hand. "No food poisoning. I make only good grub. You no have to eat any, missy."

"You gimme that," Molly said. "I didn't say *you* gave him the poisoning. Who knows where he got it from." She snatched up two sandwiches and carried them to the table where whiskey served as water, and Molly was making certain she got her share.

Loo Han Ling set the platter on the table that had been cleared of the rusty armor and swords and bits and pieces of tack — all the bitter reminders of the gold that had been theirs, and then stolen from them beneath their very noses. Loo Han Ling looked with displeasure at the limp bodies lounging about the main cabin, frowned, and left them alone.

Even with every window and door open, the place smelled like the locker room of Kappy's Gymnasium where Mandell used to meet Allan Pinkerton before his employer had turned ill. Mandell took his food outside and found McPeevy feeding King Robert the Second bits of salted ham from his sandwich.

"It be good to have King Robert back. Imagine the horrid time of it he had locked up in that cubby with poor Mr. Turnbough!"

"You will spoil him."

McPeevy grinned, muttonchops bristling back. "Aye. It is too late to be worrin' about that now, I fear."

Mandell studied the walls of stone marching closer together, compressing the river ahead. It was getting late in the afternoon, and the boat would be pulling into shore soon — before what little shore remained disappeared completely against sheer walls. Captain Patronoff would not be one to take his boat into the likes of that without the sun to show the way and knowing he had a full day to make the run through to the other side.

"Isn't it beautiful, and thrilling? I can almost feel the power of the river," Rose said at his side, and when Mandell looked over, her eyes were ahead, wide with fascination.

The tone in her voice said she had decided

on a truce — if perhaps only temporary. But that was better than out-and-out combat.

"Yes, indeed. And more than a little dangerous."

She looked at him, eyes bright. "The danger is what's so thrilling, Mr. Mandell." She gave him a curious smile and left him standing there wondering exactly what she had meant by that.

"A feisty lass, that one is. Bonny too."

Mandell almost said "Aye," but caught himself and merely nodded his head, watching with a growing admiration as Rose Haven strolled along the curve of the railing and disappeared around the starboard side.

28

Harrison Mandell was beginning to appreciate nighttime on the Colorado River, if for no other reason than that after the sun finally flared and spent itself against the western edge of the bluffs, the torrid land cooled down enough for him to enjoy a cup of coffee — and he did enjoy his coffee. Even the stout variety the deckhands boiled on shore, after wood for the *Bad Water*'s voracious boilers had been collected and hauled aboard, and a cook fire lighted.

Loo Han Ling did the cooking for them, but she left the coffee making up to the men. Coffee was not her strong suit. Tea she could brew to perfection, but her coffee either came out thin brown water or gooey black tar. She told Mandell the previous night that she had quit trying a long time ago. She had no use for coffee, a harsh American drink, and wished in her heart that she and her husband had the money to return to China where the tea was beyond compare.

The talk by the campfire revolved mostly around two subjects, with a third cropping up now and then. The lost gold was still foremost on everyone's mind, and speculation and suspicion over its disappearance brought nerves near to the surface. Turnbough's mysterious illness and death was very nearly as urgent as the lost gold. Suddenly every little twinge or gas bubble that pinched the gut was cause for concern.

They worried to a lesser extent about the Indians and their dead comrade, and what the Quechans intended to do about that. Some contended that the old chief might attack, but Captain Patronoff dismissed the notion with a gruff wave of his arm and said he understood the chief well enough to not fear reprisal. The old Indian was interested in money and making a sweet deal, and if the savages did show up again it would be with stealth, to steal the gold that had already been stolen. Not with firearms.

The conversation quieted and the sounds of the night flowed back in. Mandell poured himself another cup of coffee from the black pot canted in the coals and studied the band of stars that arced across the sky. Alf Danderfault began telling a story about hunting polar fox in Norway. Since Mandell had already heard the tale, he took his cup up the gangplank and climbed to the hurricane deck for a wider view of the dark river, the high bluffs, and the flickering of the campfire down on the shore where an occasional word spoken louder than the rest made itself heard.

In the darkness the rushing river sounded angry. Light from deck lamps showed upon it here and there in swirling and quarrelsome glimpses, and revealed the boat in disjointed bits and pieces, as if the entire contrivance was nothing more than the scattered parts of a child's puzzle.

Behind him, a burning hurricane lamp inside the wheelhouse sketched out the shape of Tommy Morgan hunched over, working at something. Probably jotting down notes on the river in his black book. He was a diligent pilot, and Mandell figured Morgan deserved better than the Colorado River.

Footsteps scraped the stairs. McPeevy's tattered bowler hat appeared first above the deck, and then the rest of him.

"I saw ye come on up," McPeevy said, setting the valise at his feet. "I was a wee bit cramped and crowded down by the fire."

"Looks like everyone needed to get some solid ground beneath their feet after the last few days we've had on this boat."

"Aye. I'm beginnin' to think ye had a bonny idea when we first arrived. Renting a couple horses and riding to the mine would have gotten us there days ago — what with waiting for this boat, then running aground twice so far, stopping to dig up gold what disappeared almost at once, then burying poor Turnbough."

Mandell laughed. "Where's your sense of adventure?"

"It got all used up on the train trip west from Kansas City. Saints, I will never know whatever made me accept a job in a place like this. Aye, the wages were more than fair, but now I understand it was all a bribe. No one in their sane mind would venture into this godforsaken wilderness for a penny less!"

McPeevy stopped, then glanced around as if suddenly aware of some change and said, "There is something different here and I ca'na put a finger on it."

"No mosquitoes?"

McPeevy blinked. "Aye! That be it. Saints, this is the first time since I stepped off the train that I did'na feel like I was bein' eaten alive."

"The water is too swift here. No place for them to breed."

"Is that what it be?"

Mandell noticed the lamp being snuffed in the wheelhouse. Tommy Morgan closed the door behind him and walked with the shuffling gait of a man weary to the bone — beaten insensible by the heat and the bugs, and the bucking current against which he had manhandled the boat's helm all day. If it had been a tedious day for crew and passengers, it must have seemed doubly so to a man with Morgan's job and responsibilities.

Morgan saw them standing there and altered his steps. In the pale wash of a running light on a stanchion off the starboard side of the towering smokestack, Morgan drew up and ran slender fingers through his long gray fringe of hair and down the back of his neck. He arched and stretched.

Mandell imagined muscles groaning and a spine popping in a dozen places. The detective said, "Long day, and not a single shoal to contend with."

Morgan grinned and shoved his spectacles up the bridge of his nose. "No entertainment for the savages."

"Working late?"

"Needed to make my notes while they're still fresh." He yawned. "Reckon I'll just get me another cup of coffee then curl up for the night. Big day tomorrow."

"The Narrows?" Mandell asked.

"Not the Narrows. Nothing big about them so long as I keep to the middle of the channel. Got one place where the channel is only nigh onto a boat's width across, but it's a short run, and so long as we don't meet with another boat coming down there won't be any problem. No, the big event of the day is that we come to the end of our haul. There will be a bath waiting, a real bed to sleep in, maybe some time to read a book before we shove off again for Yuma Town."

"Er . . . tell me about these Narrows,"

McPeevy said, "and if ye do meet another boat?"

Tommy Morgan shrugged it off as nothing. "Then one of us stops and backs out to give the other passage. The general convention is the boat heading upriver, in our case that will be us, reverses and backs down to where we can heave over and tie up until the downriver boat passes."

"Traffic is not very heavy," Mandell noted. They had passed only one other boat that day, a tiny steamer with a single engine and no upper deck. "I don't suppose it is very likely we will meet another boat."

Morgan said, "There aren't a whole lot of people this far up. The army's got a couple boats they run, and we meet them occasionally. But even military traffic is down now that the only active fort in the area is Fort Whipple, and like I told you before, it's clear beyond the Bill Bill River. They got to convoy to a landing, and that in itself accounts for most of a day's journey. Just the same, they make more use of the river than most civilian concerns."

"Tomorrow we will make the mine!" McPeevy said, his vigor suddenly renewed.

Morgan grinned. "Well, in this business I give no promises. But barring shoals or snags, or a breakdown in the engines, yes, we should reach the *Mina del Agua Mala* sometime late tomorrow afternoon."

"And not a moment too soon either," the Scotsman said with feeling. "Did ye hear that, King Robert?" McPeevy bent to lift the tomcat from the valise. "Tomorrow it's dry land and a firm footing, it is —"

The crack of a revolver shattered the peaceful night sounds.

McPeevy winced and glanced up from the valise.

Mandell had ducked instinctively. In an instant he assessed the damage done to himself, discovered to his relief that there had not been any, and immediately peered out into the darkness.

"Saints, now what is goin' on? The Indians?"

"I don't know." The surge of adrenaline slowly ebbed away, and his tension eased. "Maybe someone got careless."

There was commotion down by the fire as men looked about, some hunched down, some stalking back into shadow.

Mandell said, "Let's go see." Then he spied Tommy Morgan sprawled on the deck, not moving. The detective turned the man over, felt the warm moisture upon the pilot's chest, thick and sticky to the touch. He searched for a pulse, and after a few attempts shook his head and looked up.

McPeevy's face was white as new piano keys, and his mouth and eyes made big circles beneath the dark bowler. "Is he dead?"

"He's dead."

"Saints!" McPeevy seemed frozen in his shoes, shaking. King Robert leaped from his arms to the deck and trotted off into the shadows.

Patronoff herded them into the main cabin — every single man and woman — and started one by one demanding where each had been when the shot was fired. All had unimpeachable excuses, of course, which didn't surprise the detective, although some stood uncorroborated.

Mandell paid close attention not to what was being said but to how it was being said, and when the questioning ended and nothing had been accomplished, he broke a heavy silence with a question of his own. "Did anyone happen to see a muzzle flash?"

It seemed an obvious query, but plainly one that had not occurred to anyone else to ask.

Molly said she was certain it had come from across the river. Alf Danderfault thought the shot had come from a rise not far away. Darlinda just knew it was the Indians out for revenge. Chan and Loo Han Ling did not see the muzzle flash at all, but they both agreed the sound had come from upriver.

A deckhand, Dandy Waller, thought that Alf might be correct 'cause he too had caught a glimpse of it out the corner of his eye, and it had indeed come from either the rise, or a jumble of rocks just below it.

Mandell grabbed up a lantern.

"Where are you going?" Patronoff demanded.

"To take a look at those rocks. Two men claim the shot came from that direction. It's the best lead we have."

"Lead?"

Mandell frowned, his irritation coming to the surface. It was impossible to police one's tongue constantly. He said impatiently, "What would you call it?"

"We'll wait until daylight," Patronoff decided.

"You may do as you wish, Captain, but I intend to investigate those rocks now."

Patronoff narrowed an eye irritably at the detective then jammed his cigar between his teeth and lifted another lamp off its stanchion. "Then I'm comin' with you. Everyone else stay aboard."

Rose Haven fixed her hat firmly upon her head and positioned herself at Mandell's side.

"I said *everyone*."

"No thank you, Captain. People tend to die on your boat. I think I shall be safer at Mr. Mandell's side."

Molly made a disgusted grunt. "Not me. I ain't moving my derriere from this here cabin until we reach the mine tomorrow. And I ain't chancing the food neither," she added, slanting her view at Loo Han Ling. "This has become a boat of death and I want no further part of it."

Her girls agreed and secured themselves in chairs on either side of their madam.

"Saints, methinks the lady is right," McPeevy moaned. His face had regained its color, mostly due to the whiskey he had inhaled upon being delivered down into the cabin. Up on the hurricane deck immediately after the shooting his feet had grown leaden soles, and it had taken two strong-armed deckhands to get them moving.

Alf said, "Captain, you want I to come along?" The Norwegian accent was suddenly more pronounced than it had been. Mandell figured there was a hint of nervousness getting in the way of his usual control. Alf had been a hunter in the Old Country and his skills might be useful, but Captain Patronoff nixed the request and handed Alf the Winchester he had brought along.

"You stay with the boat. I'd feel better knowing I got someone aboard what's armed and I can trust."

The three Mexicans, who until this point had remained aloof and silent in the background, glanced up now. Edwardo instantly read the suspicious gleam in Patronoff's eye. His own scowl slowly eased into a grin. "Your boat, she's in good hands, *Señor* Captain. Me and my *amigos,* we take very good care of her."

Felix and Ramon averted their faces to hide chuckles.

"I wouldn't trust you to guard my anchor chain, let alone the whole boat. Matter of fact, I wouldn't be surprised to find you and your friends didn't have a hand in this. You spent a powerful lot of time up in the wheelhouse with Tommy, and I find that mighty suspicious now."

Edwardo stood off the corner of the table and came over. His fist dropped to the polished grip of his revolver.

Patronoff wasn't intimidated.

Mandell slipped his hand casually under his coat and watched.

"*Señor,* I did not kill the skinny *hombre.* I will not stand here and take your accusations at myself or my *amigos.*" His eyes had turned cold, like lifeless embers, and a dangerous and deadly calmness came to his voice. "But if you wish to know if I can kill, then continue on and see. I am a man of patience — but not too much."

"I will heave you and your mangy friends off this boat if I so desire," Patronoff shot back. "Your revolvers and your rifles do not frighten me." He was not armed, but Mandell had no doubts the man could carry out his threats, even if it killed him to do so.

"You may so try anytime, *Señor* Captain."

Alf was tensed, ready to defend his captain, and in these close quarters it would be more than Patronoff or Edwardo who got hurt. Mandell reached out an arm and stopped the burly man's advance. "Captain. Perhaps you ought to put this off until after we locate the one who killed Morgan." He nodded around the crowded room at the suddenly stricken faces watching for Patronoff's next move. "A lot of people might get hurt."

Patronoff drew up, his big frame vibrating with anger, realizing slowly what an impetuous act might cost at this moment.

Edwardo grinned and said, "Take your time, Captain. It is never good to be in a hurry to die."

Patronoff said, "We will continue this when I return." He glanced at Mandell. "Come along then, and let's see if there is anything out there to put an end to this mystery." Patronoff eyed Edwardo one last time, then wheeled away and stomped out the door.

Mandell eased his hand from under his coat, looked the room over grimly, and followed Patronoff out into the night with Rose at his side.

29

Half an hour earlier the site around the campfire had harbored more than a dozen people, and perhaps half that number of different conversations all being conducted at the same time. Now only the rasping chirps of crickets and the deep-throated bellow of spadefoot toads — and the searchers' own footsteps — disturbed the quiet of the night.

At the river's edge the *Bad Water* stood like a bulwark against the dark water, spattered here and there with lamplight. The bright windows of the main cabin ringed her middle like a necklace of light.

Rose spoke softly in the dark at his side, as if the night had ears and she didn't want it privy to what she was saying. "What are you looking for, Harry?"

Harry. That had a nice ring to it coming from Rose. For some unexplainable reason Harrison Mandell at once felt taller, and broader . . . and happy. He reined his thoughts back to the job at hand and said, "If we are lucky we might find a footprint. If we are very lucky we will find some piece of evidence that will point to the killer."

Ahead and to his left Patronoff stopped and turned, lifting the lamp over his head. "And the truth is, this will turn out a mammoth waste of time while on board my boat the killer remains."

Rose said, "What reason would anyone have to kill Mr. Morgan? He always stayed sort of separate from everyone else, kind of alone, with his nose in a book more often than not. So quiet — except when he got drunk last night. . . ." She stopped suddenly and said, "You don't think the Mexicans did this because of what Mr. Morgan said to them the other night?"

"I'm thinking exactly that." Patronoff had resumed the lead. The ground climbed beneath their feet, and the rocks that both Danderfault and Waller claimed they had seen a muzzle flash from loomed suddenly overhead. "And I think they done in Turnbough too."

"How?"

"Knocked him on the head and stuffed him in the closet. They must have stolen the key from my cabin so's the marshal couldn't get out if he woke up."

Rose shuddered. "He must have died a horrible death, not being able to breathe because of his allergy to cats. And then messing himself like that . . ." She suddenly hugged herself as if the night had turned frigid and looked at Mandell. "What do you think?"

Mandell lifted his lamp to view the top of the rocks. "I think I need to climb up there and take a look. Hold this, please."

"You're being evasive again." She took the lamp while he followed a ledge in the rocks and in a moment was standing atop them. He reached down for the lamp and handed Rose up with him at the same time.

Rose brushed at her skirt then looked out. The *Bad Water* rested at her moorings not far off.

"Seventy-five feet, I'd call it," Mandell said, sensing the question that was in her thoughts.

"That's not all that far. Even a mediocre marksman would have no trouble hitting poor Mr. Morgan. Even I have hit targets at that distance." Rose sighed and turned to study the dark ground at her feet and said, "Mr. Morgan made it easy for the killer. He stood in the only spot of light up on the top deck."

"It's called the hurricane deck, miss," Patronoff said impatiently from below.

She looked down. "I thought it was called the texas."

"The *Bad Water* ain't got a texas. This here is the Colorado River, ma'am. Ain't the Mississippi!"

"I stand corrected."

Patronoff held his lamp low and kicked around the tufts of stiff brown grass. It was plain he didn't expect to find anything and considered the entire effort a distraction and a general waste of time.

Between the rocks and boat the detective could just make out the campfire, its embers still burning red, partly hidden by the dark terrain. Mandell considered the lay of the land while Rose took the lamp and searched the ground. There were several ways for a killer to leave this position and make his way back to the campfire unobserved, especially after the shot had driven everyone to cover. Anyone coming in out of the dark would naturally be assumed simply to be emerging from cover.

He hunkered down and said to Rose, "Please bring the light near."

The ground emerged from the darkness. He brushed aside trampled bunch grass and frowned.

"What is it?"

"Too rocky for a print to show."

"Told you it was a waste of time," Patronoff said.

"Have you found anything down there?"

"No."

Rose said, "We don't even know for certain the shot came from here at all."

Mandell stood and studied the boat again, lifting an arm out straight to line up with the drop of light on the hurricane deck. "I think we can safely say it did."

"Is this something you learned in mining engineering school too?" she asked innocently, but with a bit of vexation coming through.

He grinned. "Like I told you, we get a very liberal education these days."

"You can be most infuriating."

"And you are lovely when you get angry."

"Enough of that up there. I'm going back to the boat and wring the truth out of them Mexicans. Wasted enough time out here in this foolishness."

"I shall return with you, Captain," Rose said, her sudden annoyance at Mandell thinly disguised.

"We will all go back," Mandell said.

In the darkness his foot struck something hard that reflected the lamplight when it skittered beneath the tangled vines growing up a nearby rock. "What do we have here?" he said, bending for it.

"What is it?" Rose asked as he rose.

Mandell grinned and placed the heavy revolver in her hand. "The murder weapon, I would venture."

"You found it?" Patronoff sounded truly amazed, and in a moment he had scrambled up the rocks to join them.

"Yes, he did!" Rose's irritation of a moment before vanished. She showed the revolver to Patronoff. In the flickering light the burly man's face went rigid, the cigar drooping in his lips. He took it from her mechanically and turned it over, not believing what he was seeing.

"What is the matter?" Rose asked.

Patronoff stood mute, a figure of black marble, eyes like saucers.

Mandell said, "The captain is speechless, Rose, for you see, the murder weapon is his very own revolver."

The first words from his mouth after he had recovered enough to speak were "Them damn Mexicans! They stole it from my cabin. They had to have!"

"Why?" Mandell asked simply.

Patronoff glared. "Well . . . well, don't you see? They're trying to frame me."

"Again, why?"

He stammered, then his dark eyes flamed in the lamp light, suddenly intense. "Them Mexicans, they must have stole the gold. They figure there ain't no way they was going to get away with it with so many men aboard, so the first one they killed was Turnbough. Get rid of the lawman first. Make it look like an accident so as to throw suspicion off of them.

"Then they figure to kill Morgan, and make it look like I done it. That way they'd get rid of two of us at once, Morgan dead, me in chains until we reach dock."

Rose said, "It's all coming together. It's so plain. The captain has it figured out, I'm sure of it." She looked at Mandell for reassurance, and he gave her back a face that told nothing of his own thoughts.

"Well?" she insisted.

"It doesn't make sense, Rose."

"Why not?" Patronoff rumbled.

"Yes, why doesn't it make sense?"

"With Morgan and the captain gone, who would pilot the boat? And if they did not intend to take the boat any farther upriver, why kill anybody? Why not just disappear one night? That would be easy enough. And since we are throwing out unfounded accusations anyway, consider this: The captain was the one who thought coming out here to look for clues was foolishness."

"I was wrong."

"It was he who wanted to end the search before we had found anything."

"I didn't know —"

"And why did he insist on coming with me in the first place when I could have done very well on my own?"

"To see to it you didn't get into any trouble," the captain shot back angrily.

"To make certain we didn't find the gun?" the detective suggested instead.

Patronoff shook with rage.

Rose was confused and shifted her view between the two men. "That . . . that makes sense too." She clearly did not know what made sense anymore.

"And since we are casting out accusations like bread upon the water, consider this: The captain and Turnbough were old friends — well, at least they had been friends a long time ago. Friendly enough to embezzle forty thousand dollars from the Keokuk and St. Louis Packet Company."

Rose staggered back. "Is that true?"

"You stinkin' meddler. Turnbough was right about you." Patronoff lunged, but the revolver came up in Mandell's hand, cocked, and the captain drew back.

"So, it was you all the time," Rose cried, shrinking from the fierce bearded face.

"No, it wasn't him at all. Patronoff is innocent — at least of the crimes done here."

She looked at Harrison Mandell, startled. "But you . . . ?"

He grinned in the darkness. "All that I said about Captain Patronoff is true, Rose. But the captain did not steal the gold, and he did not kill Turnbough or Morgan."

Patronoff eyed him, confused, and said, "It's true, I had no part in it."

"I never thought you did." Mandell turned the revolver in his hand and offered it to Patronoff. "And, if I haven't missed my guess, you're going to be needing this."

After a moment of hesitation Patronoff took the revolver, broke it open to check the loads in the cylinder, then snapped it closed. He studied Mandell in the dark.

"Who the hell are you?"

The confusion left Rose's face in an instant and she said, "It was the Mexicans after all."

"No, it was not them either. They are here for an entirely different reason, and we best get back to the boat before it's too late."

30

The deck of the *Bad Water* had a stillness about it that made Mandell's skin crawl. Through the heaps of cargo, the detective saw the lighted window of the main cabin, but the room might as well have been abandoned for the absolute silence of the place.

The silence instantly alerted Patronoff too. "Something's happened," he said at once, and plunged up the steps. Rose gathered up her skirt and climbed after him. Mandell lingered a moment in the shadows, but whatever the trouble, playing cat and mouse was a fool's game. He always preferred to be in the thick of it. His jaw set. He loosened his Colt Lightning in its shoulder holster and put his feet to the steps.

Patronoff's bulk very nearly filled the doorway when Mandell stepped inside. Rose had come to a halt not far from the captain, and her hands were now covering her mouth. Across the room Edwardo stood off the corner of the table with the Springfield rifle over his left arm directed at Patronoff in a casual manner that would be a deadly mistake to misinterpret. A grin of quiet contentment hitched up on the Mexican's dark face.

Mandell slipped into the room alongside the captain.

"Back so soon?" Edwardo asked. "Much luck, no?"

Patronoff began to speak. Mandell cut him off. "No luck at all. Guess we'll never know who killed Morgan."

Rose's face registered surprise, but she kept her thoughts to herself.

"Too bad," Edwardo said, but the matter had no more significance to him than losing a round in a friendly game of poker.

Mandell shifted his view. No one in the cabin was moving, no smiles . . . except on Edwardo's face. Even Ramon and Felix radiated a tension so heavy it might have sunk the boat had it been granted shape and mass.

"Felix," Edwardo said, "take the captain's gun."

Felix's fingers tightened about his revolver. He approached with the caution of a man who expected resistance. Patronoff offered none. Felix yanked the revolver free of the captain's belt, then he glanced at Mandell.

"I have no weapons."

"Search him anyway," Edwardo snapped.

Felix opened Mandell's coat and removed the revolver that hung under his arm.

"Wonder how did that get there?" Mandell said, seeing the sweat stream from the Mexican's face. Felix had none of Edwardo's self-assurance, and that was something to keep in mind.

"Come in, come in," Edwardo said now that they were disarmed. He smiled and hooked his arm at them, suddenly in a gregarious mood. There seemed a considerable number of firearms present, all of them in the hands of the Mexicans.

Alf Danderfault had hung back in a corner. Now he stepped out into the light, where his swollen eye and the careful manner of his walk spoke plainly of what had transpired while they had been out hunting up clues.

"I couldn't stop them, Captain," Danderfault said, swaying a trifle when he stopped and sounding disgusted with himself. "I tried."

"Don't worry 'bout it," Patronoff rumbled low in his throat, and to Edwardo, "What am I to assume here? Are you shanghaiing the *Bad Water*?"

Edwardo cocked his head. "I do not understand this word — shanghaiing?"

"Are you seizing, commandeering, *stealing* my boat?"

He understood that and grinned. "*Sí*, I am shanghaiing your boat, *Señor* Captain."

Ramon slipped into position by the door. Mandell kept him in view while Felix slid up near the starboard side of the cabin, putting the wall to his back and gripping Alf's Winchester as if any moment he expected someone to take it away from him. Edwardo returned to his place on the corner of the table, his left foot solidly planted upon the floor, his right swinging the tall black boot in the casual manner of a man who might have been surrounded by dear and loving friends instead of men who would dearly love to run a sword through him.

That notion caused the detective suddenly to glance at the pile of conquistador armor and weapons in the pile by the corner.

"For what purpose have you taken this vessel?" Patronoff's voice pulled his attention back.

"To go upriver." Edwardo feigned surprise to have to explain it.

"You were already doing that."

"*Sí*, but now we do it the way I want to do it."

"What the hell does that mean?"

The grin slipped from Edwardo's face, an abrupt hardness taking its place. "It means, *Señor* Captain, that you will have your men at once put wood into the boiler. How do you express it? Get up a head of steam?"

"Now?"

"*Sí*, now."

Patronoff glared at the Mexican and in an instant it struck him. "You intend to put out into the river tonight! I will not do it!"

The Springfield came up menacingly.

Patronoff jammed the cigar into his mouth

and narrowed an eye at the Mexican. "You're loco, you know that? We'll run into a snag for certain. Rip her hull wide open. Then where will you be?"

"At the bottom of the river, *Señor* Captain." Edwardo laughed, the rifle nudged in Patronoff's direction. "Order your men to do it now! I wish to not harm you or your passengers. There is no need to do so. But if I have to, I will. With no hesitation."

In half an hour the boiler had been fired up. Its open mouth roared, and hissing steam escaped the engine vents by the paddle wheel. A shower of red sparks lent an eerie cast to the night sky above the *Bad Water*'s twin smokestacks. Patronoff glowered out through the window into the night, his fingers curled around the spokes of the big wheel. Every running lamp had been lighted. A lamp hung off the bow. Still there was not enough illumination to pilot a boat by, especially in this swift water. The jagged spires of rocks could be seen scattered out into the channel. It was a fool's trip, and Patronoff knew it, and he wished that Tommy Morgan was standing behind the helm instead of himself. Tommy knew this section of water. If any man could have gotten them through, Tommy could have.

"Now, *Señor* Captain, we will go."

Patronoff frowned. "You know this is suicide."

"Then we will all die together." The rifle barrel was hard against his spine. Patronoff yanked the cord that rang a bell down in the engine room and shouted into the speaking tube.

"Alf, get her hot, we are pulling out."

"Aye, aye, Captain" came the hollow reply.

Patronoff glanced once over his shoulder at Edwardo, put the bandit out of mind, and concentrated fully on the black river ahead.

The *Bad Water* shuddered to life, the big wheel digging powerfully into the river, shoving her ahead, first in jumps and jolts, and then more smoothly as the boat picked up speed. Patronoff cranked the helm hard to port to gain the center of the channel, and he squinted at the black water visible only a few dozen feet ahead of the bow. In places the sheer rock walls of the canyon stood so close to the water that the running lights showed its dark looming surfaces.

Patronoff could hear the men below heaving fuel into the boiler. Although the night air had cooled as it does in the desert, he suddenly found himself slinging the sweat from his forehead to keep it from filling his eyes.

Felix pushed away from the cabin wall where he'd been keeping a split watch — one eye on the passengers and another out the window at the shadowy landscape slipping by. He said something to Ramon at the door.

Ramon nodded his head and Felix went outside. Afterward Ramon redoubled his guard, the Winchester cocked and ready to be put into use at an instant's notice.

McPeevy gathered up his valise and carried it to the door. "Saints, ye du'na think ye can drop me off on shore and I will wait for the next boat to come along?"

"Sit back with the others," Ramon said.

"Aye. I di'na really think ye would go for it anyway." McPeevy returned to his chair.

Mandell inclined his head at Rose and said quietly, "I need to find a way out of here."

"Don't we all," she commented, equally quiet.

He grinned. "Well, how about one at a time?"

"Whatever happened to women and children first?"

"That applies only to sinking boats. And then only when at sea."

She gave him a smirk and said, "What do you have in mind?"

"I don't — at least not yet. I need some kind of diversion."

Below the table his shin got an urgent pointed-toe jab. He glanced over to read the look in Molly's eye. She'd been following the conversation, and now he hoped he had rightly interpreted the almost imperceptible nod of her head.

Molly said something to Darlinda and then

to Betty. The two women stared a moment at the madam and then at each other. Mischievous grins emerged as their eyes met, conferred, and then agreed wordlessly.

Amazing, thought Mandell, recalling the unspoken communication he had observed between Darlinda and Molly back in the barroom of the Southern Pacific Hotel. He wondered vaguely if clairvoyance was in some manner a prerequisite for working in their profession.

Betty stood, strolled over to the bar, and poured herself a tin cup of whiskey. She drifted over to Ramon then and asked if he'd like a drink.

"No, *señorita*," he said, but the bandit showed no immediate desire to send her back to her chair.

Betty shrugged her shoulders and tipped up the cup. When she lowered it she patted her forehead with the back of her hand and cursed the heat. She left the Mexican and stood by a window looking out, sipping the whiskey. In a few minutes Betty returned to the bar. As she snatched up the bottle for a refill, Mandell caught the quick twist of her wrist that dumped what appeared to him to be an absolutely full cup of whiskey over the far corner of the bar.

In plain view, Betty made a display of carefully refilling the cup, and then she started at it all over again, first peering outside, then strolling near to Ramon, giving him a smile that each time appeared more careless than the previous.

Molly leaned over the table and said under her breath, "Give it a few minutes."

Mandell nodded. Rose was watching Betty with open curiosity, and perhaps, he suspected, a bit more understanding than she cared to let on.

Darlinda rose out of her chair and filled a cup for herself. She said, "If we are going to smash ourselves to bits on the rocks tonight, I don't want to be sober either."

"Now you girls take it easy with that devil brew," Molly admonished. "It'll make you see double and feel single!"

Betty giggled. A pretty good tipsy sort of giggle, Mandell thought. "Why, Molly," she said overly loud and careless, "I am single!" She and Darlinda got a big kick out of that.

At the door, Ramon grinned briefly, but the Mexican wasn't yet ready to be distracted.

Mandell figured this was going to take some time to work itself through. He glanced back where the curtain across the women's quarters was still in place, half drawn. The door there was closed. Unfortunate. At least there was no lock to have to contend with.

31

The wailing rent of wood and straining timbers shrieked like a ricocheted bullet through the *Bad Water* as the steamboat skidded off a submerged rock and jerked halfway across the channel.

"Damnation all to hell!" Patronoff roared, fighting the helm. He lurched around and the rifle jerked up in Edwardo's hands. A deadly reminder. The captain eyed it, then the man behind the trigger. "Let me drop anchor and wait until daylight. You're gonna get us all killed, dammit!"

"No. We must go farther, *Señor* Captain." Edwardo's usual calm had vanished, replaced by a temper with a hair trigger.

"Why?"

"Because I say we do!"

"You fool," Patronoff rumbled, turning back to the inky water where even the scant moonlight didn't reach.

Edwardo glanced at the open book of charts at Patronoff's elbow. "Where are we now? Where exactly?"

"How the hell should I know? Can't see but a dozen yards in any direction."

"The Narrows. How far?" he demanded.

Patronoff shifted his view for a moment, saw the intense glare in the Mexican's eyes. "The Narrows? Now is a fine time to be worryin' about that."

"Answer!"

"Like I said, I do not know exactly." Patronoff bit down on his cigar and got the tip glowing bright enough to show his own face in the reflection off the black glass. "If I was to guess, I'd say they're just ahead not more'n two or three miles. And it is about time you started to worrying. Chances are I ain't gonna get us through in one piece."

Edwardo glanced at Felix who had joined him in the wheelhouse a few minutes earlier and snapped a command in Spanish.

"Here, what's all that about?" Patronoff demanded. He received no reply, but observed that Felix had suddenly acquired a bad case of the jitters.

"*Sí, Edwardo,*" he said, rushing away. Patronoff saw Felix hurrying down the stairway before losing sight of him. He frowned at himself in the window and said, "What the devil you three got up your sleeves?"

Edwardo did not answer.

They were fairly well drunk by the time Felix poked his head through the door and spoke to Ramon.

"You want a drink, darling?" Darlinda slurred.

Felix ignored her. He had no time for such antics. In rapid-fire Spanish he said what he needed to Ramon.

Mandell leaned near Rose and quietly asked, "You understand any of that?"

She nodded her head. "Felix says the time has come. He is warning Ramon to be ready as there is liable to be some commotion." She looked at him, bewildered. "Time has come for what?" The bewilderment on her face turned to suspicion. "You know, don't you? You know what it's all about!"

Mandell shot a look at Molly. "I need to get out of here. Now!" he whispered.

She nodded and gave a long look to the girls draped about the bar, her eyes compressed, and then she lowered her head briefly.

At the doorway, Felix snatched the lamp off its stanchion and disappeared into the night. Ramon resumed his watch, now hardly able to restrain the new and sudden tension that radiated into the room.

Darlinda went into her act.

"Whew, it's gettin' hot in here," she said, running fingers through the wilted mass of florid hair and tossing her head back. Her fingers worked the buttons on her shirtwaist and in a moment her neck lay open, exposed in a most brazen manner as she fanned herself.

"I'll say so," Betty agreed, and faster than most women could slip off a jacket, Betty had her shirtwaist unbuttoned down to the top of her skirt, revealing the white chemise and the healthy swell of her breasts beneath it.

"I'm still hot!" Darlinda complained.

They had managed to catch Ramon's attention.

Mandell's too.

Get your mind back on business. The women were doing their part, now it's time to do yours.

Rose's face had taken on a flush. She glanced at him and must have perceived his interest in Betty and Darlinda's capering about for immediately a scowl crossed her face.

He grinned back at her and glanced over his shoulder to measure the distance to the rear door.

"Here, lass. You shouldn't be a-doing that," McPeevy advised, his voice quavering.

"Mr. McPeevy," Betty said, impassioned, "aren't you hot in that shirt?" She staggered over to fiddle with its buttons.

"Now stop that, lass!" he said, batting away her hands, almost losing the valise he'd lifted to his lap.

Darlinda giggled. "You know what I'd like to do right now?" she said, playing out the drunk routine like an old gaslight pro.

Betty turned away — to McPeevy's great relief. "What?"

"I'd like to take a nice cool swim."

"Me too!" Betty was suddenly bubbly.

"Now, girls," Molly said mildly. "It's dark out there, and besides, the captain would never stop the boat to let you swim."

"Oh, I bet he will," Betty said playfully, and in the next instant both women had unbuttoned and dropped their skirts. Beneath them the crimson of their crinolines matched the glow McPeevy's cheeks had taken on. The crinolines hit the floor, and the next moment they were wiggling out of their drawers.

Ramon's eyes had grown too large for their sockets.

"Girls! Girls!" Molly admonished. "Stop that right now!"

"Oh, my God!" McPeevy croaked. His feet had begun tapping the floor like a drum roll as he squeezed the valise upon his lap.

Mandell shot a glance at Ramon. The girls had managed to capture the Mexican's full attention, and he was clumsily fiddling with the knot in his sweaty bandanna.

Rose's attention was riveted too despite herself, and her view kept leaping back to Mandell as red spread up her cheeks and under her chin.

"Oh, no!" McPeevy groaned.

"Aye, Chihuahua!" Ramon howled.

A hip bustle that Darlinda had been swinging dropped to the floor. Long pink legs stretched out: a magnet to the men's eyes. Chan Loo began a patter in Chinese, and Loo Han Ling clasped her hands over his eyes.

In a single move Betty grasped the hem of the chemise in both hands and lifted it over her head, and in the next instant she was stark naked, stretching languishingly toward the ceiling and saying how good it was to finally feel the evening air all over, and now let's see if the captain won't stop the boat for us.

Molly leaped up. "Enough is enough. Where is a blanket?"

"There is one back by the cots," Mandell said.

Suddenly Darlinda was in Ramon's arms, and that seemed more a surprise to the bandit than to anyone else. The rifle was clumsily set aside and his hands moved all over her, and she encouraged more. Molly dove for a blanket while McPeevy moaned and squirmed in his chair, and in that instant when Molly tossed the blanket over Darlinda and Ramon, Mandell slipped out the back door and was gone.

He swung over the railing and dropped lightly to the main deck, drawing up in the shadows to listen for any sounds of pursuit. But he had landed near the engine room, and the slamming of the pistons and hiss of escaping steam had masked any sound he might have made. In a moment he grabbed a hog-ring on the deck and lifted the panel.

The detective had searched out the stern hatches to the cargo hold earlier that afternoon, making sure he could find them in the dark if he had to. He opened the hold only wide enough to ease himself through, hoping any stray light would not be seen below. If he had not missed his guess, Felix would be down there right now working his way back from the bow hatch.

In a moment his eyes grew accustomed, and he saw the light ahead. It appeared far off, but it could not have been more than fifty feet, tossing shadows about the hold as Felix pushed it ahead of himself.

The nervous shadows steadied after a minute and the sound of the bilge plug access hatch being lifted out of place reached Mandell's ears above the pounding of the engines. He moved forward quickly, feeling his way through the dark, keeping the light ahead as a point to aim toward.

It was impossible to avoid every obstacle, but he managed not to crash into anything that gave his presence away. When Mandell did stop, the rush of water under the hull beneath his hands and knees was an urgent reminder of the peril the boat was in.

Through the gloom of the cargo hold shot the squeal of metal against metal, as if the wrenching loose of a rusty screw that hadn't been turned in many years.

Mandell resumed his stalking advance. Ramon would have realized he was missing by this time — if the bandit hadn't been subdued in the confusion when Molly heaved the blanket over him. He could only hope he had. Just the same, time was paramount, and his first job was to stop Felix.

Mandell eased through the cargo and flattened to the floor. Beyond the crates he saw Felix heaving against a long iron bar that he'd slipped through the ring atop the bilge plug. Straining against years of rust, Felix rooted the heel of his boot in a gap in the floor plank and was putting his weight against it.

The plug turned and metal sang out. Felix stopped, removed the bar, reset it in the ring, braced himself, and had at it once again.

Mandell gathered himself in like a compressed spring, timing his move to the next squeal of metal. Then overhead a rifle fired, and again a second shot cracked.

Felix looked up from his work, startled, and in that instant he glimpsed Mandell ready to lunge.

Mandell sprang from cover as the Mexican reached for his revolver.

The revolver exploded in the cramped cargo hold. But an instant before, Mandell had taken hold of Felix's wrist, and the bullet

282

carved a splintered furrow from the deck overhead. His momentum carried them both backward, crashing into crates that tumbled to the floor. The two men rolled across the floor, struggling for control of the revolver.

Mandell swung the Mexican's wrist against a deck support and the revolver skittered away in the darkness. Then a fist like a knotty club connected with his jaw. Mandell's head slammed the floor, stunned. He twisted it aside and Felix's next swing pounded his fist into the floor.

The Mexican yelped, and in the flickering lamplight Mandell saw Felix's teeth take a determined set as his arm cocked back.

Mandell came up with a knee. Felix jackknifed and grasped his ribs. The detective twisted out from beneath him and, still on his knees, jabbed out. But in the cramped space he had no freedom of movement and the punch missed. Felix came back with one that connected and again the detective went over.

Stunned, he shook his head. When his eyes focused he saw that Felix was casting around for the missing revolver. The Mexican spied the weapon and dove for it, but Mandell put himself in his way and the two men butted together like combatting bighorn sheep.

Mandell's fist connected solidly this time. Felix staggered back and knocked his head on the deck. The detective scrambled to his haunches and threw a second punch.

Felix dove aside at the last moment, and when the Mexican came back around he was grasping the long iron bar. He swung out. The bar whistled in the air over Mandell's head. He swung it again, smashing the lamp and sending a spray of blue flames throughout the cargo hold.

The cramped space instantly plunged into darkness. Mandell heard the Mexican nearby, and then here and there pockets of light returned to the hold again, growing brighter, flickering red.

Felix spotted the detective and swung the iron bar. It smashed a wooden crate and lodged there, and as he struggled to wrench it free a flash of yellow in the growing orange and red light streaked out and caught him on the chin.

His head snapped back as if a mule kicked back. Mandell heaved back and the knuckle dusters streaked out again. Felix spun around and collapsed.

Mandell sucked in a deep breath, tasted smoke in the air. A dozen small fires were slowly eating their way up the cargo and licking hungrily at the underside of the main deck. The hold grew bright. He slipped off the brass knuckles and dropped them into his pocket, grabbed up Felix's revolver, tucked it into his belt, and, hooking his fingers into the leather of the Mexican's vest, dragged the unconscious man forward.

After knocking open the bow hatch, the detective lifted Felix through it and in the next moment was making his way around piles of cargo back to the main cabin.

32

Mandell dove through the open door with the revolver cocked and ready. When he hit the floor and rolled to the side, he swung the weapon around, but Ramon was nowhere in sight. Rose glanced up from the floor where she and Loo Han Ling were working to stop the blood that had turned the sleeve of Chan's shirt crimson.

"Chan tried to apprehend the bandit," Rose said briefly.

"How is he?"

"He'll live. I'm not so sure about Mr. McPeevy though."

It was then that Mandell noticed Molly and Betty bent over the Scotsman. His shirt had been ripped off his chest, and the two women were using bandages torn from their clothing to try to stop the bleeding from his chest. King Robert had retreated to the top of the bar, near the ceiling, his fur like a bristle brush.

Betty had slipped into her chemise, he noted, and Darlinda was off to the side quickly buttoning up her skirt. Molly called for water, but no one seemed to know where to find it.

"Where did Ramon go?" Mandell asked. There was nothing he could do here, and he still had two more bandits to stop.

"Once he discovered you were gone he went looking."

The detective said, "Make preparations to get Chan and Gilligan off the boat. There is a fire in the cargo hold."

The general confusion at once doubled. Mandell plunged toward the rear door and came up short when the report of a rifle exploded on the deck below.

He crouched into the darkness and climbed over the railing again, as he had done not ten minutes earlier. Somehow it seemed longer than that to the detective as he made his way forward. He pulled up at the boiler. Its iron skin glowed a dull red from the fire inside, and near it Alf Danderfault was sprawled in an expanding pool of his own blood.

Mandell knelt and saw at once that the big Norwegian was dead. He glanced around for Ramon. Already the fire below was showing through the cracks in the deck.

A shower of splinters exploded from the wood near his head. He wheeled and discovered the Mexican working the lever of the Winchester. Mandell fired. Ramon staggered back, caught himself, dropped the rifle, and disappeared down the dark gallery.

In a leap, Mandell was in pursuit. He fired a second time as the bandit wheeled around the corner and into the engine room.

The detective's pulse thumped in his ears, almost masking the sound of the steam engines.

From back by the turning paddle wheel came a single shot, as if Ramon intended only to dispatch an obstacle in his way, and then all was quiet again — except for the even rhythm of the engines. Mandell went swiftly down the gallery, his senses suddenly keen and aware of everything around him: the splash of water against the hull, the engines beating strongly, the odor of gunsmoke lingering in the air. His brain ran down a check list. He was using Felix's revolver, and it had been fired once by its owner. Mandell had fired twice. That meant there were either two or three bullets left — depending on whether Felix had loaded it to six, or carried it with the hammer down on an empty chamber, which was the custom of men who understood these weapons.

At the corner he drew up to listen, but all he could hear were the engines cycling just beyond the wall. On the floorboards was a spot slightly darker than the surrounding wood. The detective stooped and ran a finger through it. Warm, sticky. He didn't have to see the color to know what it was.

Mandell spied a second splash of blood, at the threshold of the engine room door and moved up alongside it. He drew in a breath, knowing full well what awaited him on the other side, and plunged through.

In the blackness two pistols spit fire at each other, and then a man staggered and fell back against the boat's throttle.

"What the blazes is going on down there?" Patronoff barked, turning to face head-on the rifle in Edwardo's fist.

Edwardo's dark eyes shifted as he too tried to determine the reason for the gunshots and at the same time keep Captain Patronoff under control.

"Just steer the boat!"

"No! No more, damn you! We are all gonna die anyway, either by your guns, or by running up onto the rocks —"

His words were cut short by the two shots that rang out so close together they sounded as one. An instant later the *Bad Water*'s giant paddle wheel slowed and came to a halt. At once the excess steam shrieked like a death wail from the escape pipe.

"What did you do?" Edwardo demanded as the *Bad Water* slowed against the current.

"Do? I didn't do anything."

"You have stopped the engines."

"I can't do that from up here."

"Start them again, quickly!" Edwardo fought down panic. "If you do not I will kill you now!"

"I told you I can't. Got to go down to the engines to do that."

The boat came to a stop in the water, and then the current picked her up and shoved her backward. In the darkness she careened sideways. Patronoff leaped for the helm to try to straighten her, but with no power the boat drifted helplessly, driven on by the river, and gaining speed.

"The engines! Start the engines!"

"I can't, damn you son of a bitch! Don't you understand? I can't do that from here. I'll have to go down to the engine room!"

"No! No more of your trickery." Edwardo's dark face froze in a mask of rage as he brought the rifle up.

Patronoff saw the end was near. He was not a man to go without a fight. Without warning he lurched at the Mexican, and at the same time the rifle exploded. The bullet shoved Patronoff back and around. The big man broke out the wall of windows before regaining his footing. Blind rage filled him, and he dove for Edwardo's throat as the bandit grappled for the revolver at his side.

The two staggered out of the wheelhouse, stumbled down three short steps, and rolled to the deck. Patronoff's fingers clenched Edwardo's throat. The Mexican fumbled his revolver from the holster, brought the butt of it up into Patronoff's chin.

Stunned, the captain reeled back. Edwardo

rolled from beneath his grip, gasping, put distance between himself and Patronoff, and cocked the revolver.

Shaking off the blow, Patronoff lifted himself to his knees and glared at the Mexican and his gun. "Go on, damn you. Shoot your heart away. We are all finished here anyway."

As he spoke the boat bumped a rock, groaned, shifted around, and slipped sideways down the river.

Edwardo took aim —

A shot erupted in the night and then a second. Edwardo slammed to the deck. He tried once to lift himself and fell back.

From the shadow behind the wheelhouse Harrison Mandell stepped out and tossed the Mexican's revolver aside. He helped the captain to his feet.

"You've been shot."

Patronoff winced, the pain only now making itself known. He looked at the arm and then clamped a massive hand over the wound. "It's nothing," he said, then with urgency: "We need to get an anchor overboard before we break up."

"Too late for that. There's a fire burning down in the hold and we're going to the bottom."

"She's lost then." No sentimentality, only a statement of fact. After all, Mandell figured, it was only a little boat on a miserable river. He wondered if the captain would have felt any different if this had been the Mississippi instead.

"There are wounded below. We've got to get them off."

"I heard the shots," Patronoff said, coming out of his thoughts and heading down the steps after Mandell.

The *Bad Water* rammed another rock, wood splintered. She listed steeply to port and spun around in another wild circle. Down on the main deck fire was eating through the planks. Mandell caught himself on the railing, grabbed Patronoff, helped him up the sloping deck and into the main cabin.

"We've got only one dinghy aboard. Load the wounded into it and we'll put it over," Patronoff said, assuming his rightful role as the man in charge. "The rest of you will have to do for yourselves. Anyone here don't know how to swim?"

No one admitted that they didn't.

Mandell dropped down next to McPeevy. "How is he?" he asked Molly.

She shook her head grimly. "He needs a surgeon's help. Nothing we can do for him."

The boat shuddered and lifted on its starboard side. The table and baggage went sliding across the floor. The armor and ancient weapons clattered like so much scrap iron to the port side of the cabin.

"Abandon her!" Patronoff shouted.

Darlinda screamed.

The bow tilted down and the rear of the cabin rose.

Rose was suddenly at Mandell's side. "I'll help you with Mr. McPeevy," she said.

Another lurch and the *Bad Water* grounded with a moan as a section of her hull opened up. A lamp broke from its stanchion and crashed to the floor. Instantly flames shot up the dry timbers.

The river dragged her back out into the water, bow heavy and sinking. Rose took McPeevy's weight onto her shoulder, and between her and Mandell they hauled him to the door. The boat spun, tossed them against the main cabin wall. Below, fire was working its way up to the boiler deck. The gallery was red with flickering light, and the heat was like an iron upon them. They pulled themselves uphill until they reached the dinghy. Everyone lending a hand, they got McPeevy aboard, and Chan climbed in with him under his own power.

"You too, Captain," Mandell said.

"I stay with my boat until all hands are safely off her."

"We are all that's left!"

Patronoff ignored him.

A rock ripped open a gash in her starboard side, and the *Bad Water* lurched in a new direction. In the light of the burning deck, Mandell watched the last of the hands leaping overboard into the swift water.

"Help me lower her off," Patronoff shouted.

Mandell grabbed up a line. Rose, Molly, the girls took hold of the lines too. Loo Han Ling climbed aboard with her husband and McPeevy.

"Someone will have to help row it ashore," Mandell said.

"They'll have to take their chances alone," Patronoff shouted back over the sudden explosive hiss of the boiler where the rising water had reached. "Hurry it up before she blows!"

The dinghy descended to the water. Patronoff opened a knife and cut off the lines and the current swept the little boat away. "Now everyone, over the side!"

Molly, Betty, and Darlinda leaped. Rose hesitated. "Aren't you coming?"

"I'll stay with the captain."

"But the boiler?"

Mandell took Rose up in his arms against her protest and the next instant her flailing arms and legs beat the air, and then the water below.

"You need to abandon ship too," Patronoff said.

"Not until you leave."

"Dammit, I'm the captain! I got to make sure everyone is safely off."

"Everyone is off! It's just you and me, and you're bleeding too badly to carry on like this any longer. Come on, I'll jump with you."

"No!" He looked at once fierce and then suddenly there was acquiescence in his face. "I don't intend to leave, Mandell." He laughed briefly and said, "A captain is supposed to go down with his ship."

Mandell heard the rising pitch of steam as the water seeped into the boiler. "We don't have time for this maudlin bullshit! Let's get the hell out of here!"

"Hear me out. You are right, of course. I don't know how you found out, but you did. I am guilty of embezzling cash from the steamboat line I worked for, though I can't imagine where you got the figure of forty thousand dollars from." He laughed. "It was more like five thousand. Five or forty, it makes little difference. The fact is, I'm guilty, and I can never go back."

"We can discuss this later."

"No we can't, dammit. I'm telling you, I ain't leaving. Don't you understand? I can't go back to the Mississippi, and I'm tired of living without her. When we found the gold, well, for a moment I had new hope. I figured I could finally pay back the money I stole, clear my name, perhaps work the river again before I die. But now the gold is gone. My share would have surely covered what I owe . . ." He stopped, and then, "This is a better way. You know the truth, so does Miss

Haven. Soon the word will get back East. I'm too old to start running from the law, Mandell." His black eyes reflected the fire below. "Now that I explained it, and I ain't one to often offer explanations, you get out of here. Get off this ship of death before she blows us both to hell."

Mandell grimaced. "All right, if that's the way you want it. I'll go alone."

"It's the way I want it."

Mandell turned toward the railing, and then with the suddenness of a prizefighter, he rounded and hit Patronoff with a blow that sent the big captain to the deck.

The detective gathered him up, straining under the massive weight, and stepped to the edge of the deck.

At that instant the boiler blew.

33

The *Bad Water* had come to rest in a scattering of rocks near the Arizona shore of the Colorado River. Her bow smashed in defeat on the bottom of the river, her stern lifted indecently high, exposing both paddle wheel and rudder to the air.

The sight was almost sad, and for an odd moment Harrison Mandell imagined they should be opening Patronoff's Bible and saying some words over her. He thought back over the night — the fire, the explosion that had thrown Patronoff and himself clear of the wreckage, the confusion afterward as he and Rose had searched the shore for survivors . . .

He yawned and watched the campfire lose its brightness against the morning dawn. When it had grown light enough to see by, he saw that they had come ashore less than half a mile from the Narrows. A mist hung over the water. It would remain only briefly before the sun gained its full strength and burned it off.

The *Bad Water* was scorched down to the waterline. Only her hindquarter had been spared. He glanced over to the others. Captain Patronoff and Chan Loo were both finally asleep, and Mandell's heart was like lead when he thought of McPeevy. So far the Scotsman had survived — only just. He needed a surgeon desperately, and there appeared little hope of finding one here, marooned on the wild banks of the Colorado River.

Rose Haven stood wearily at the campfire. It had burned low, and now that daylight was here there was little need to keep it stoked up, for they had no food to cook, and nothing to boil water in, although the wounded desperately needed some. She came over and sat next to him on the rock, ready to drop from exhaustion, needing a good long sleep.

"How is the adventure going?" he asked her, marshaling a grin.

"I just don't understand any of it."

"Any of what?"

She shook her head. "Any of this." Her arm swept the campsite and the wreckage of the *Bad Water.* "Why? For one thing, what *were* Edwardo, Felix, and Ramon up to?"

"Oh. That's an easy one."

She looked at him, too tired to hide her irritation. "Maybe for some of us," she said.

Mandell pointed at the high cliffs above the Narrows. "Take a look up there. What do you see?"

She shaded her eyes against the rising sun. After a moment Rose picked them out. "There are men up there," she said, surprised. At the dying campfire Molly and her girls turned and stared up at the bluffs. "Who are they?"

"Revolutionaries. Up from Mexico. Remember, you told me about them yourself after overhearing their talk. I just fitted all the pieces together. My guess is that their charismatic leader, the next president of Mexico — or so they had hoped — was apprehended by the army up above the border. The cavalry has him and at this very moment is transporting him by steamboat down to the Territorial Prison in Yuma."

She studied him. "How could you know that from what little I overheard?"

He smiled tiredly. "I don't know. It's the way my brain works, I reckon." He stood all at once and studied the river. "I'd say that's the cavalry coming now." A smudge of smoke was making its way around a bend in the Narrows. "A little late, but better late than never." Mandell grinned. "And if Edwardo had been successful in his plan, the *Bad Water* would be sitting on the bottom of the channel right now to bar their way, and the cavalry would be trapped there while above the Mexicans picked them off at their pleasure."

She studied him. "Who are you?"

"Come on, let's flag that boat down."

* * *

The *George Clinton* was a little sternwheeler hardly a hundred feet long. She pulled into shore above the smoking remains of the *Bad Water*. When her gangplank had been lowered, an armed squad of troops secured the area while the captain, a young man with a scraggly red beard and pale skin that looked vastly out of place in this sun-ravaged country, stepped down.

"Trouble here?" he asked.

Mandell said, "We've had our share, Captain. Could use the army's help." He indicated the bluffs. "But first you might want to take precautions. There are about twenty Mexicans up there, and my guess is they would dearly like to relieve you of your prisoner."

The officer was momentarily taken aback by the detective's knowledge of the army's business, then he ordered his men to secure the boat. Afterward he said, "You have wounded?"

"Three. One serious."

"We have a field surgeon on board." And with that the captain called the doctor down, but the medical officer was already on his way, with an aide and an armful of supplies. The captain turned to Mandell, "You in charge here, mister?"

"No, sir, Captain Patronoff is, but he's been wounded."

"Patronoff?" The cavalry officer glanced at the smoldering remains of the steamboat out on the river. "The *Bad Water*?"

"What's left of her."

He studied Mandell a moment then said, "How did you know we were carrying a prisoner?"

"Too long a story to tell now."

"I see. And your name, sir?"

"Harrison Mandell."

"Harrison Mandell?" The captain's eyes became suddenly focused. "I have a telegram for you. Actually I was supposed to deliver it to the *Mina del Agua Mala*. Wasn't sure how I was going to get it there since I was heading in the wrong direction. Thought I'd send it up with Captain Patronoff when I arrived at Yuma Town."

"A telegram for me?" Mandell considered telegrams that came in the middle of a mission suspect. Only one man knew how to find him.

"It's on board. I'll get it in a moment." The captain looked at the crew and passengers stretched out around the campsite. "You folks must be hungry. All we have is hardtack, but you're welcome to it." With that he called up to a soldier on the *George Clinton* and immediately the man carried off a small wooden barrel about the size, Mandell thought, of the keg of beer still down in the secret icebox in the *Bad Water*'s cargo hold.

Rose said, "I'll take that," and wrapped her arms about the heavy barrel . . . and that's when it struck Mandell — like a freight train!

"Where are you going?" Rose asked him when he suddenly leaped about.

"I've been so stupid! I'm going back to the boat."

"There's nothing left of it."

"We'll soon see," he called over his shoulder as he waded out into the water to the wreckage of the *Bad Water*. The paddle wheel served as a convenient stepladder to the charred deck. Among the smoking timbers he located the stern deck hatch, heaved against the warped and twisted wood, and hauled it open.

The fire was dead below what remained of the deck, drowned by river water. The back of the hold was dry and tilted at such an angle the detective had to brace himself as he worked forward. The water began a few feet before he reached the secret icebox. He wedged himself between the box and a deck upright and opened the lock with his picks.

He dragged the door open, heavy against the weight of the water against it. Everything inside had piled over to one side, and the odor of beer spilled from the box. Mandell grabbed up the beer keg, wrestled it into his arms. It was mighty heavy, and he labored uphill to the stern hatch. He set it up on the deck and was about to pull himself after it when a tiny sound at the far end of the submerged boat reached his ears. Mandell turned back and waded deep into the hold.

Harrison Mandell carried the weighty barrel of Coors beer off the boat, holding it high on his shoulder as he waded back to shore. Atop the keg a wet and frightened cat rode with its claws buried in the wood and an unceasing mournful wail near Mandell's ear. He reached land and King Robert the Second departed the barrel in a grand leap that carried him a few dozen feet up the shore.

Mandell set the keg in the sand by the smoldering fire. Rose studied him without saying a word, and Captain Patronoff, who by this time had been awakened by the surgeon, looked at it with a mix of confusion and pain.

"Where the hell did that come from, Mandell?"

"Among your private cache of beer, Captain."

He was stunned. "How did you — well, never mind. That's impossible! I have never ordered down any keg beer from our Colorado mine. Always bottled." He narrowed an eye at Chan Loo, and the little Chinese man began to squirm under the burning stare. "This your doing, Chan?"

Mandell noted that both Chan and Loo

Han Ling were suddenly quite anxious.

Then a movement caught his eye.

The old chief and his men rode into camp and reined to a stop a healthy distance from the armed soldiers.

"Ho, Captain!"

Both Patronoff and the young cavalry officer looked over. The chief gave them a broken-tooth grin. "We make deal now?"

Darlinda didn't stir, too weary to care.

"The day this Colorado River freezes over solid, Chief, that's the day we'll make a deal!" Patronoff wheeled around to Mandell. "You got something on your mind, mister. I can read it all over that smirking face of yours."

"The first time I saw this keg, Rose was with me. She moved it aside easily. I should have suspected it right off considering it had never been tapped. The second time, when I moved it, it was heavy. Something had been put inside." Mandell lifted a boulder up over his head and smashed the barrel. Conquistador gold spilled onto the ground, and beneath the gold was neatly packed bundles of United States Postal money orders.

"Glory!" Patronoff roared, and Mandell saw new hope explode in the man's eyes. Everyone gathered around the gold — everyone except Chan and his wife. They would have liked to have quietly departed, except Chan's wounds prevented that, and really,

Mandell mused, where in this godforsaken land could they run to?

Patronoff glared at Chan. "It was you!"

"It was both of them," Mandell corrected. "They took the gold in the confusion when Olley came aboard. My guess is that they have been stealing regularly from the mine, and when the gold came within their reach they saw their ticket back to China. Loo Han Ling would like nothing more than return to China. Isn't that right?"

She glowered at him.

Not only had he found the gold, but he seemed to have solved the problem of the missing money orders from the Bad Water Mine. He grinned, thinking that Allan would approve of the neat way he wrapped it up.

Rose said, "But Loo Han Ling was in tears when the gold turned up missing. I saw her."

"Loo Han Ling had been an actress in the Beijing Repertory Company, in China," he said. "An actress who can't cry on cue isn't much of an actress, is she?"

Rose was stunned.

Patronoff turned stormy and glared at the couple. "Then you two are responsible for the marshal's death, and Morgan's too?"

Chan's eyes popped. "No! No killee nobody! Nobody but Indian!"

"You're a liar!"

"The Loos are telling the truth," Mandell said. "The murders — well, that's an entirely different story." And he looked over at Darlinda.

Darlinda stood up, suddenly wary. She cast about for some means of escape, and then her eyes brightened and she announced happily, "I've come to a decision, everyone. I've decided to go with the chief's son after all!" She grinned and took a step backward. "Who knows, it might be a kick in the pants. I ain't never had me a buck Injun afore." Another step to the rear. Olley began to grin and squirm in his saddle — Darlinda had on only a skirt and chemise and looked tantalizing despite the wear and tear of the journey. "You all don't have to worry 'bout me. I'll write to you, Molly . . . Betty. Let you know how everything is going." She grinned widely. "Well, it's been . . . interesting."

"Captain," Mandell said, addressing the cavalry officer, "I believe you have the authority to arrest, do you not?"

"I have the authority to take into custody," he said.

"The difference is a moot point. Please take that woman into custody."

"For what reason?"

"Murder."

This stunned the officer. Darlinda wheeled and she dove for the Indians' ponies, but the old chief wanted none of her trouble now.

Two soldiers took her arms and escorted

her back to the captain. "Please explain," he said.

"Yes, please do," Patronoff seconded.

Mandell said, "First off, Turnbough did not die of his asthma as everyone assumed. It's what Darlinda had hoped you would think, that's why she threw the cat in with him. The marshal died of arsenic poisoning. She had given it to him the night before, probably mixed with the tequila he had been drinking. But she had misjudged the dose and it only made him sick the next morning. Later that day she administered the fatal dose — probably right in the storage room where we found him. Then she locked the door and most likely threw the key overboard. If you had examined the body afterward, you would have seen the red rash that had formed on his arms and the jaundice coloring."

Patronoff scowled, glanced at the woman and back at Mandell. "Where did she get the arsenic?"

"From your cabin when she retreated to it the day Olley came aboard. You took the precaution to keep the medical supplies there, and I presume you likely kept other dangerous chemicals there as well." Patronoff's face told Mandell he was correct. "She also took your revolver and the key to the storage compartment door at the same time."

"What about Morgan?"

"Morgan was an accident. Darlinda had been shooting at McPeevy. The distance was long — for a revolver — and she missed when Gilligan stooped to pick up his cat."

The eyes of those gathered there turned toward Darlinda as if under the control of a single thought. Her face had lost all color.

Rose said simply, "Why?"

Mandell made a wry smile. "Darlinda is wanted for murder back in the States. Molly knew about it, didn't you?" He looked at the madam, who had turned pale. "And she tried to cover for her, but killing was easy for Darlinda, too easy for her to keep from showing her true nature. She had killed her husband back in Kansas City. She killed Turnbough because she feared being a lawman, he'd discover that she was wanted."

"And McPeevy?"

"Ah, now that was sheer coincidence. McPeevy had the misfortune of having known the woman years ago. She didn't remember him until she heard him playing his bagpipes, then it all came back. She knew that he knew of her crime, and tried to kill him for that."

The cavalry officer ordered Darlinda taken aboard. McPeevy went up next on a stretcher, Patronoff and Chan followed, Loo Han Ling going along with a soldier taking up the rear.

Mandell gathered King Robert the Second into his arms. As he started up the gangplank

Rose Haven was suddenly at his side, and he felt good.

"Who are you, really?"

He smiled thinly, wearily. "Who do you want me to be?"

"Harrison Mandell . . . himself."

"Mr. Mandell," the cavalry officer said, "here is the telegram I told you about."

Mandell passed the cat to Rose, took it, and broke the paste seal:

DEAR HARRY STOP ALLAN PASSED AWAY THIS MORNING STOP YOU WERE ON HIS THOUGHTS TO THE LAST STOP JUST THOUGHT YOU SHOULD KNOW STOP

LOVE JOAN

"Is something the matter, Harry?" Rose asked him.

Harrison Mandell caught himself an instant before the moisture came to his eyes. He blinked it away, smiled valiantly at Rose.

"No, nothing," he said. "Nothing is wrong."

He crumpled up the telegram, shoved it into his pocket, and went aboard.

About the Author

Douglas Hirt writes out of a fondness for the frontier West and the people who rose up to meet its challenges. Crammed with action and authentic detail, his novels are rivaled only by masters of the genre. Douglas Hirt lives near the base of Pikes Peak, Colorado, with his wife, Kathy, and their two children, Rebecca and Derrick.

The employees of Thorndike Press hope you have enjoyed this Large Print book. All our Thorndike and Wheeler Large Print titles are designed for easy reading, and all our books are made to last. Other Thorndike Press Large Print books are available at your library, through selected bookstores, or directly from us.

For information about titles, please call:

(800) 223-1244

or visit our Web site at:

www.gale.com/thorndike
www.gale.com/wheeler

To share your comments, please write:

Publisher
Thorndike Press
295 Kennedy Memorial Drive
Waterville, ME 04901